"So, you're looking for a man."

Lyle's voice was openly derisive.

"Actually," Jessica responded blandly, "what I'm looking for is a *husband*. I want a civilized relationship with someone who accepts marriage as a business arrangement."

Lyle looked at her thoughtfully. "Then you're talking about the type of marriage that could be set aside when it was no longer viable?"

"Well...yes," she agreed stiffly.

"You're young, only twenty-six. What happens if you fall in love?"

He was watching her carefully. Jessica had a strange desire to convince him that she would make him a good wife. "That will never happen," she said coolly. "You see, I just don't believe in 'falling in love.'"

But for the first time in her life she wasn't sure....

FROM THE EDITORS

Penny Jordan is one of our favorite authors, and a favorite of readers around the world. Her books are as genuine, as full of life and as keenly observant as she is, and she has a knack for capturing characters that touch the hearts of women everywhere—in all cultures and languages.

Other books by Penny Jordan

HARLEQUIN PRESENTS

MIRA

Penny Jordan

Research Into Marriage

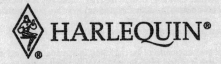

HARLEQUIN®

TORONTO • NEW YORK • LONDON
AMSTERDAM • PARIS • SYDNEY • HAMBURG
STOCKHOLM • ATHENS • TOKYO • MILAN • MADRID
PRAGUE • WARSAW • BUDAPEST • AUCKLAND

ISBN 0-373-83419-5

RESEARCH INTO MARRIAGE

CHAPTER ONE

JESSICA GRIMACED with exasperation as her phone rang, disturbing her train of thought. This was the fifth time it had rung this morning. How on earth was she going to get even the research done for this new book, with all these interruptions?

As she reached for the receiver she remembered that her sister had told her she ought to employ a secretary: with two definitive books in her particular field published already she was regularly in demand to speak at seminars and universities. Initially she had quite enjoyed these opportunities to lecture on her work, but now she was finding she was having to cut down on these activities. There was only three months to go before the draft of her third book was due at her publishers and as yet she was only half way there.

Rather abruptly she spoke into the receiver, her frown deepening as she heard her sister's anxious voice on the other end of the line.

'Jess...please...you've got to help me...I just can't cope any longer. David's behaving so oddly.

I'm sure there's someone else.... He's so...so indifferent towards me...'

The mixture of pity and irritation churning inside her was not an unfamiliar one. Jessica had never wanted her elder sister to marry David Chalmers; right from the start she had recognised him as a weak, vain man who would soon grow tired of her sister's open adoration and start to stray.

But what she had *not* bargained for, was that David would want to stray in *her* direction! Listening to her sister's outpourings with one ear, she started to doodle absently on the pad in front of her, her frown deepening when she realised that what she had drawn was a caricature of her brother-in-law's boyishly handsome features. Angrily she stroked through the sketch. The desire that David insisted he had for her was not something she returned. On the contrary she loathed the man; found him vain and shallow to the point where her irritation often threatened to boil over, but so far she had always managed to keep her temper under control, more for her sister's sake than her own. Andrea had fallen head over ears in love with David during her university days when she had been one of his students. Delicate, blonde and rather fragile as Andrea had been in those days it was easy for Jessica to see why her sister had appealed to David, especially when one took into account the rather substantial amount of money both she and Andrea had inherited from their father on his death. Oh yes, David had always had a healthy respect for money and for all the comfort it could provide.

It was Andrea who had bought the large five-bedroomed house they lived in, on the better side of town; and it was Andrea's investments that provided the money for the new BMW every two years, and private school for their son William. But the most damnable thing of all, at least as far as Jessica was concerned, was that when it came to revealing to her sister her husband's inadequacies, her hands were tied.

From the moment her first book had started to be acclaimed a success David had been a nuisance. At first she had found his over-attentiveness in public, his constant claims to being what he termed 'her only real male relative', and his equally unacceptable physical overtures towards her whenever they met, more of an irritation than a threat.

She had presumed that Andrea, having gone ahead and married the man, was well aware of her husband's weaknesses; and where better for a man with David's taste for a succession of adoring, nubile young women in his life to be employed than at a university as a lecturer?

But as Jessica had discovered over Christmas, her sister seemed to have a facility for blinding herself to her husband's true nature.

When she had come upon Jessica struggling in

David's arms, in the study, where she had gone to borrow some books, Andrea had immediately leapt to the conclusion that Jessica had been the one doing the inviting. For weeks afterwards there had been a coolness between the sisters, which Jessica suspected had affected her more than it did Andrea. Although Andrea was the elder, in many ways it had always been she, Jessica, who had been the stronger of the pair for all the three years' difference in their ages.

It had been Andrea who almost collapsed following the death of their father from a heart-attack, her grief driving her to the edge of a nervous breakdown, even though neither of them had seen him since his divorce from their mother ten years previously.

Jessica had been stunned to discover that they had been included in their father's will along with the two children from his second marriage. Following the break-up of their parents' marriage her father had emigrated to Australia, where he had done very well for himself financially.

Jessica had gone to his funeral: Andrea had not been well enough to make the flight, but Jessica had felt totally out of place there; a stranger who had no right to be amongst the grieving family of a man whom she barely knew.

It had been following her father's death, as a catharsis for the guilt she had unexpectedly felt, that she had written her first book; basing it on research which she had spent almost two years gathering. The book dealt with the problems arising from the break-up of family units and its effect on the members of those families and its publication so soon after she had obtained her degree in psychology had caused quite a stir.

She had followed it up eighteen months ago with a more detailed study on the long-lasting effects of childhood events, including parental divorce, on children, and that book too had been received very well. She had, or so her publisher claimed, a facility for explaining the most obscure technical data in a way that made for easy reading and absorption.

However, as Jessica had discovered, success brought its own problems, and in her case the most unpleasant of these was the decidedly unpleasant knowledge that her brother-in-law appeared to have switched what shallow affections he had from her sister to herself.

Had Andrea been a stronger character Jessica could simply have told her how unwelcome her husband's advances were, but then had she been a stronger character, she would have never married a man like David in the first place.

Physically as well as emotionally Jessica found that he repelled her. It had come to the point now where if he so much as touched her she could feel her body stiffening, his effect on her much the same as that on a cat whose coat has been stroked the wrong way. If it hadn't been for Andrea she would have had no compunction in telling him exactly what she thought of him, but that was not possible.

Her sister, now in her third month of a very precarious pregnancy, had developed a paranoid fear of losing her husband, which seemed to focus on what she believed to be Jessica's desire for him, and David, recognising the weapon his wife had put into his hand, was taking every opportunity of using it.

It was useless for Jessica to tell her sister that she had no emotional interest in David. Andrea would not be convinced. Jessica suspected that Andrea did not want to be convinced, because privately she was well aware that David was unfaithful to her, and for some reason she preferred to believe that this unfaithfulness involved her own sister rather than someone else—a stranger whom she could not manipulate by using the emotional tie between them.

'Jessica...promise me you won't see him again...I know you saw him last night...he was out until gone two...I rang you...you were out too... Please don't insult me by lying about it...I know how you feel about him.'

Holding on to her self-control Jessica muttered beneath her breath, 'I wish to God you did.' Her fingers gripping the phone were damp and she could feel the tension spiralling up inside her. She knew quite well that Andrea needed medical attention, but

David, because it suited him to pretend otherwise, refused to consult their doctor about her deteriorating mental condition.

Only last week when Jessica had pointed out to him how debilitating and dangerous her sister's neuroses were becoming, especially in her pregnant condition, David had merely shrugged his shoulders and suggested slyly, 'Well, since she already thinks we're having an affair, why don't we?'

His vanity and cruelty both sickened Jessica; sometimes she felt as though she were caught in a miasma of deceit from which there was no escape. She personally loathed lies and deception. It had shaken her world to its foundations when their parents split up, even though her mother had explained carefully to her at the time that it was a mutual decision.

Certainly as far as divorces go it had been reasonably amicable. Her mother had re-married nine years ago when Jessica started university and now lived in Canada with her new husband, who had offered both Andrea and herself a home. Guy was a nice enough man; he adored her mother but, as Jessica had learned from her own research, what a child wanted, no matter what the impracticalities and impossibilities as far as the adults were concerned, were for its two parents to be together, and since all adults carry within them the ghost of the child they had been, the feeling of desertion and betrayal that comes from being a child of a broken marriage never completely fades. It can be rationalised away, analysed and accepted, but something of it is always there.

She had no delusions about herself, or others; David wanted her now because she had something Andrea did not have—academic success. It would suit David very nicely to be the husband of a successful woman, but not for long. A man of David's low emotional stature would very soon find those small cruel ways of undermining such a wife; those tiny, unkind gibes in public that she had so often heard exchanged by other couples. But there was no question and never had been of her marrying David, or anyone, come to think of it, she thought wryly. Her life had been so busy that there had never been any time for her to form a lasting relationship, and for her, marriage was something that had to be based on more than mere physical lust. Love, or what commonly passed for it, was no basis for security; better to marry for political, financial and practical reasons; to make a contract with another person and stick to it than to risk so much on the mere irrational whim of one's hormones!

And that was to be the basis of her next book. At the moment she was deeply engrossed in her work on this book and what she had researched so far confirmed her views that so called 'arranged' marriages, provided they were motivated purely by a parental desire to achieve the best possible chance of happiness and contentment for a child, had more chance of succeeding than any others.

It was to be a radical and challenging book when it was finished, and Jessica had no doubt that she would receive an awful lot of flak about it, but she was sincerely convinced that she was right in her views.

In a surprising number of cases though, she had discovered that love had grown from these 'arranged' marriages, and although she was rather loath to admit it, that rather upset her theory that 'love' was not a necessary ingredient for success.

'Jessica, are you listening to me?'

Andrea's voice was high-pitched with hysteria. 'Promise me that you'll give David up, that you won't see him again.'

This was getting ridiculous. She fought down an urge to tell her sister not to be so stupid, and instead said patiently, 'Andrea, David means nothing to me.'

'You're lying. I know he's seeing someone and if it isn't you then...'

The high-pitched voice was suddenly silent, tension humming along the wire as though her sister had suddenly discovered a chasm had opened at her feet. As indeed she probably had, Jessica thought tiredly. Poor Andrea. If she was to accept that her sister was not having an affair with her husband then that meant she must accept that he was in all probability having one with someone else, someone she could not control so easily. And it wouldn't be his first affair, Jessica thought angrily.

'Andrea, try to calm down,' she said quietly. 'Think of the baby.'

It was obviously the wrong thing to say as it provoked a storm of weeping and hysterical demands that 'no, *you* think of it, think of it when you're making love to *my* husband,' and then before Jessica could retort the phone was slammed down.

Jessica knew what that meant. Tiredly she stood up, flexing her muscles, where they were strained from tension. A tall woman, with long legs and full breasts above a very narrow waist, she had a shape which she remembered from her teens as being distinctly out of fashion. That view had stuck, and now she tended to wear clothes that concealed rather than revealed her almost lush femininity.

Her hair was thick, with a natural curl to it, a deep shade of copper; her skin almost translucently pale, except in summer when it freckled. Her eyes were a curious shade somewhere between green and gold, and depending on her mood could look either colour.

Up until the success of her first book she had disdained make-up, but several appearances on television without it had convinced her of the necessity of adding at least some colour to her pale skin, and

thanks to the make-up departments of the various
television studios she had visited she was now able
to apply it with a fair degree of skill.

She would have been openly astonished if anyone
had referred to her as looking sexy; as a teenager
she had been so conscious of the differences between herself and all the other girls she knew, who
all seemed to have fragile, slender bodies, with
thirty-two inch chests that she had firmly imprinted
on her mind as the type of women preferred, these
almost androgynous females.

David's desire for her she put down quite simply
to money, and the fact that she was indifferent to
him.

She was wearing her normal working clothes
which consisted of a track-suit and a pair of ancient
trainers. Most mornings she liked to go for a run or
a long walk before she started work, it helped to get
her mind in gear and made up for all the long hours
she spent shut up in her study. When she moved it
was with a loose strong gait that, had she but known
it, drew every male eye she passed in a mixture of
fascination and frank awe.

Now she would have to go round and see her
sister. Despite her present exasperation with her, she
was truly fond of Andrea, and if privately she
thought that her sister would be far better off without David, she was wise enough not to voice these
thoughts.

It only took fifteen minutes to drive from her flat, one of half a dozen in a large Victorian mansion with its own grounds, to her sister's house.

She found Andrea in the kitchen, her face swollen with pregnancy and tears, and genuine fear for her sister's health drew Jessica's eyebrows together in a frown.

Andrea had been warned by her doctor that if she wanted to carry her baby to full term she must rest and relax as much as possible, but that was proving almost impossible, what with Andrea's ridiculous suspicions about David and herself, and her sister's highly strung nature.

As she walked into the kitchen Jessica noticed that the date was ringed round on the kitchen calendar as being one on which Andrea should have attended her ante-natal classes, but when she questioned her about it, Andrea shook her head and said bitterly, 'How can I concentrate on anything like that when my own sister's having an affair with my husband?'

Holding her breath and slowly counting to ten Jessica sat down and said gently, 'Andrea, I promise you I am *not* having an affair with David.'

'But he wants you,' Andrea interrupted shrewdly.

It was not something she could deny. She had never been a good liar and she doubted that she could start now.

'He *does* want you, doesn't he?' Andrea de-

manded, her face flushing alarmingly as she picked
up on her sister's inability to deny the charge. She
was trembling visibly, her body far too thin and
frail. 'Why don't you find a man of your own?' Andrea demanded hysterically. 'Why must you take
what's mine? If you want a husband...'

Unable to bear the torment in her sister's face
Jessica turned away, her attention momentarily
caught by the newspaper on the table. It was open
at the personal columns and absently she noted all
the ads for potential mates both of a temporary and
a permanent nature. Apparently it was quite com-
monplace these days to advertise in this way, proof,
if she had needed it, that more and more people were
beginning to realise that it was possible to have a
marriage based on something other than mere physical attraction. Her mind once more on her work, it
was several seconds before she realised her sister
was speaking.

'Jess, please, please give him back to me.'

Andrea was crying now, ugly, gulping sobs that
shook her thin body. Jessica could feel the exhaustion of trying to cope with her sister's disturbed
mental state creeping over her. It would kill Andrea
if she lost this child; she had already had two mis-
carriages in the years since William's birth, but another miscarriage was exactly what she would bring
on if she continued to torment herself in this fashion.

But what could *she* do to convince Andrea that there was nothing going on between David and herself?

She hadn't realised she had spoken her last thoughts out loud until she heard Andrea saying thickly, 'Find a husband of your own, marry someone, Jess, and then I'll believe you.'

On the point of retorting that Andrea was being ridiculous, her eye was unwillingly drawn to the newspaper again. Who replied to these personal ads? How many of those replies were genuine ones and how many were not? *Why* did they reply? Perhaps for the sake of her research this was an avenue she ought to pursue?

Even as the denial formed in her mind Jessica found she was asking herself just how much she cared about her sister's welfare and health. Marriage these days did not necessarily involve a lifelong commitment, it could be a business arrangement— sometimes for illegal purposes such as when someone wanted to become a British citizen, or perhaps even when a husband or wife was needed for some other reason—as in her case. It might even be a way of discovering at first hand how viable her theories on arranged marriages were.

Suddenly a tiny thrill of excitement pierced her. She of course did not intend to fall in love—but if she could prove to herself that such a marriage would work, what a wonderful way of confounding her literary attackers! Dare she? Or was she being totally ridiculous?

It took her an hour to calm Andrea down to the point where she could safely leave her, but even once she was back at her desk, Jessica found it impossible to concentrate on her work. The ridiculous idea which had taken root in Andrea's kitchen refused to be dislodged. When she thought about it logically there were several advantages at present to her having a husband; most importantly it would force Andrea to accept that there was nothing between David and herself, and it would also make David realise the pointlessness of pursuing her any longer; and not just David, but also those other men who had shown an interest in her since she had become something of a public figure.

Of course she would have to make sure that legally and financially she held the upper hand, but pre-marriage contracts were not entirely unheard of these days. She frowned, startled by how much thought she was giving to what was surely a ridiculous idea.

By early evening she had completely dismissed the thought from her mind and was busily studying the notes she had made the previous summer, so that when the doorbell rang it was several seconds before the sound penetrated her consciousness.

When it eventually did she was annoyed by the interruption. But her visitor, whoever it was, seemed determined not to go away. When she opened the door and saw her brother-in-law standing outside, his fair skin flushed by alcohol, his blue eyes faintly glazed, her own narrowed in biting contempt.

'Whatever it is you want, David, I don't want to know,' she told him curtly. 'Go home to your wife.'

He grinned at her, the inane, self-satisfied smirk of a man whose conceit overshadowed everything else.

'Oh, come on Jess.' He was slurring his words, his voice overloud in the enclosed hallway, and she glanced anxiously at the other doors, hoping that none of her fellow tenants would emerge and see David standing there. But she was also reluctant to invite him in, knowing it would take her ages to get rid of him.

'You know you want me,' he told her thickly. 'Stop fighting it. It could be so good for us, babe.'

His arrogant egotism coming on top of her own tension snapped the frail cord on her temper, and before she could stop herself she heard herself saying furiously, 'You're quite wrong, David. Far from wanting you I loathe you, a fact that even you will have to accept now that I'm getting married.'

'Married!' It socked him into momentary sobriety. 'You're lying, Jess.' He said it harshly, coming towards her as though he meant to take her in his arms. 'You're not the marrying type. You never have been. You're too bloody independent for marriage. You're incapable of wanting a man—any man—to the extent that you'd marry him,' he went on, betraying the fact that he was quite well aware of how little she cared for him. 'The only thing that matters to you is your work, your research...' He paused and then stared at her, his eyes glittering with spite. 'I get it,' he said quietly. 'That's what it is, isn't it, Jess? This marriage of yours is just an experiment. A way of testing out the theories behind your new book.'

It had been impossible to hide from David what the subject of her new work was to be, and now temper ignited inside her that he should have so completely read her mind, but she toyed with the idea of denying it and telling him that the only reason she was contemplating such a course was quite simply to save her sister's health, when it struck her that it would be far wiser to let him believe what he had just said. Apart from anything else it would be a mammoth blow to his pride to know that she would marry a stranger rather than submit to him, and so with a smile that was entirely false she said sweetly, 'Yes, that's quite right, David,' and then with a slam she shut the door in his face and locked it.

Now that she was committed, incredibly she was very calm. Before she went to bed she drafted out her advertisement, keeping it as brief and general as possible, quoting merely her age and sex. It was the most quixotic thing she had ever done in her whole life, and amazingly she felt neither anxiety nor guilt at the thought of it.

THE LIFE OF A COUNTRY GP, when he was the sole doctor for a radius of twenty miles with only the back-up service of an understaffed cottage hospital behind him, was certainly no sinecure, Lyle Garnett decided tiredly as he folded his long frame into his shabby estate car.

When he had voluntarily given up the brilliant career specialising in micro neuro-surgery that had been forecast for him his friends had thought he was mad, and privately he tended to agree with them, but the involvement and commitment needed to succeed in that sort of field were not something he could give and bring up two children as well, especially not two boys as rebellious and difficult as Stuart and James.

It was because of his career that he had seen so little of them during their early years. Even before their divorce he and Heather had been living in semi-estrangement; he devoting long hours to the advancement of his career, and Heather constantly complaining about the two small children which had made the continuation of hers impossible.

The fact was that they should never have married. Heather hadn't wanted to. When she discovered that their affair had led to a pregnancy she had wanted to go for an abortion, but he had been young and idealistic in those days and he had stubbornly held out for marriage. He had loved her then, or had thought he did, he acknowledged wryly, but what in effect he had loved had been a very young man's dream of a woman, not the reality. He had wanted Heather to be the mother to his children that he himself had never known. His mother had been an actress, someone he saw very infrequently and whom he had yearned for desperately all his childhood. She had died when he was sixteen from a brain haemorrhage, and her death had sparked off his interest in medicine, filling in with a crusading and totally impractical dream of curing the world of all its ailments.

Time and reality had hardened that idealistic teenager into the man he was today, a world, and almost twenty years, away from that boy of sixteen. Now he recognised that for his own sake he should have allowed Heather to have her abortion. If he had maybe she would still be alive today...but that was an old guilt and one he had learned to live with in a way that he had never learned to live with his guilt towards his sons. He loved them but they were hostile towards him. They resented the fact that they had lost their mother and in her place gained a father who was virtually a stranger to them. He and Heather had divorced when James was two and Stuart four and Heather had died two years ago, running directly into the path of an oncoming car, having just had a row with him.

She had always had a terrible temper, something he had pushed to the back of his mind when as a young houseman of twenty-odd he fell in love with her, and when he had refused to take the children so that she could emigrate to America with her lover and take up the medical career she had been forced to abandon when she became pregnant, she had flown from his flat in such a fierce rage that she had never even seen the car.

She had been killed instantly, the driver distraught with shock; and in death she had achieved what she had not been able to achieve in life. He had had to take on the responsibility for his sons. Not that it had been a lack of love for them or reluctance to care for them that had prompted his refusal, merely the belief that their place was with their mother. But Heather had never wanted them. She had told him so often enough. And so he had had little alternative but to give up his career as a neuro-surgeon, and instead look around him for something less demanding and time-consuming that would mean he could take charge of his sons.

He had heard of this rural practice from a friend of a friend, and the local medical board had been astounded and delighted at the thought of getting such a highly qualified man for the job.

Within a month of Heather's death he and the

children were established in Sutton Parva, several miles west of Oxford, where his married sister and her family lived.

Justine had promised to do all she could to help him with the boys and had been as good as her word, but there were still problems. He frowned as he drove homewards. The boys were both rebellious and sullen; and being older than their cousin tended both to dominate and persecute him. Although he told himself that their bad behaviour sprang from insecurity and pain, there were times when he was so exasperated by them that he almost wanted to be able to resort to the old-fashioned parental hard hand in a place where it hurt the most. So far he had managed to restrain himself.

Added to all his other problems was the fact that as a widower and a doctor, not to mention what Justine called his ridiculously unfair share of good looks, he was constantly having to fend off the romantic and sexual overtures of some of his female patients.

It took him half an hour to drive home. The house he had bought from the previous doctor was large and rambling, with a garden that he made infrequent and haphazard attempts to tame.

Far from enjoying their country environment his sons never ceased bemoaning the lack of facilities. Raised as city children, even after eighteen months they were still not at home in the country. The new bikes he had bought them for Christmas were virtually unused, and obvious but nonetheless effective method of showing their dislike and resentment of him.

A large part of the problem was that Heather had never made any attempt to hide from the children how little either parent had genuinely wanted them, and they in turn were fiercely determined to show the rest of the world, especially their father and his family, how little they wanted him.

Even while he understood and sympathised with them, Lyle found they exasperated him.

He knew the moment he entered the kitchen that there had been another scene.

Justine, who like him had inherited the strong family profile and thick dark hair, was standing belligerently by the table, the silence thick and taut with angry resentment.

'I've sent the boys upstairs,' she told him without preamble. 'I had to bring them back early. They tied Peter up in the garden and built a bonfire under him. They told me they were playing at Guy Fawkes.' Her eyes darkened as she said unsteadily, 'Dear God, Lyle, if I hadn't caught them in time...'

She had no need to go on. He himself felt physically ill at the thought of what could have happened.

'I can't look after them for you any more, Lyle,' she told him bluntly. 'I know their problems aren't necessarily their own fault, but I've tried everything, and nothing works. They need someone of their own.'

She watched sympathetically as her brother sat down; a big lean man, with a shock of thick dark hair, and eyes of a vividly intense blue, who at this moment in time looked older than his thirty-five years.

She loved him and she sympathised with him, but she could not risk the safety of her own dearly loved eight-year-old any longer with a pair of children whom she frankly considered to be beyond her ability to help.

'God, Justine, what the hell am I going to do?' He looked so tired and depressed that she was tempted to retract, but she hardened her heart against him.

'Well, for one thing, this,' she told him firmly, placing a folded newspaper down on the table in front of him. 'Go on, read it,' she demanded, waiting until he raised his eyes to hers in incredulous disbelief, finely mixed with anger.

'You're seriously suggesting what I think you're suggesting, are you? That I reply to this ad from some crazy woman who wants a husband, sell myself?'

'Why not? Other people do it all the time,' she interrupted evenly. 'Only they call it self-sacrifice. You're a doctor, Lyle,' she reminded him, hoping he wouldn't guess how much she hated doing this to him. 'But how long can you go on calling yourself that? How long will it be before all the problems you've got here occupy so much of your mind that you make a mistake? A mistake that could cost someone's life?'

She was only echoing his own inner thoughts, but to do what she was suggesting! He put his hand to his forehead and found that he was sweating slightly.

'I just can't look after them any more,' Justine pressed on. 'I've got Peter to think of. They need someone of their own,' she added more gently, 'someone who can give them what you and I can't.'

'And you think this…this stranger, a woman who needs a man so desperately she's forced to advertise for one, will do that?' he demanded harshly, expelling the pent-up breath from his lungs so tensely that it hurt.

Justine lowered her eyelids so that he wouldn't see the sympathy and pain in her eyes.

'I know that after Heather you said you'd never marry again, Lyle, but the children need a mother, even if you don't need a wife. Of course, you could always marry one of your patients. Sylvia Hastings, for example.'

She saw the grimace and understood why. Sylvia was a pretty divorcee with a tendency to develop

minor ailments, and an avid look in her eyes whenever they rested on the doctor.

'She's not capable of looking after herself, never
mind two kids.'

'No, and she would demand something from you
that you're no longer capable of giving, wouldn't
she, Lyle?'

She said it quietly, hating herself for delivering
the blow but knowing she had to. After Heather's
death, he had told her that his guilt had affected him
so strongly that he felt completely unable to touch
any other woman. Physically he was as capable of
being aroused as the next man, but mentally there
was something there, stronger than that physical
need, which had destroyed his desire for sex.

'A marriage with someone with whom you can
make a proper business arrangement would solve all
your problems,' she told him quietly. 'I'm not saying that you marry the woman in this particular advertisement. But its one way of looking for someone. And to help you make a start, I've replied to
this on your behalf.'

For a moment she thought he might actually hit
her, but then the angry colour died out of his face,
leaving it white, a muscle beating sporadically
against his jaw.

'By God, Justine, you push your luck,' he told
her thickly. 'I don't want or need your interference
in my life.'

Her own anger beat up inside her, reminders of how they had quarrelled as children filling her mind. He had been so stubborn, a trait both his sons had inherited.

'Maybe not, but you *do* need my help, and it is my right to decide what form that help will take,' she told him evenly, adding for good measure, 'I've replied to the advertisement suggesting that the woman calls here to see you.' She saw his look of incredulous fury and held up her hand. 'I had to do it, Lyle. I know you, if I hadn't you'd find a way of wriggling out of it. I'm not asking you to marry the woman, not at this stage. I'm simply telling you that your children need someone in their lives that they can trust and relate to, and it seems that neither you nor I can fulfil that role. They *are* your children, Lyle.'

'Yes.'

He said it wryly, his voice heavy with acceptance, and Justine felt herself relax just a little. Knowing of his decision never to marry again she had realised what she had taken on in adopting such a high-handed course of action, but she was convinced that it was the only way to help Stuart and James. Lyle might not need or want a wife, but they both needed and wanted a mother. It was after all no worse than the arranged marriages organised by many Eastern parents for their children, and on balance these worked.

'Good.' She smiled briefly and glanced at her watch, squashing her guilt. 'I'll have to go. The boys had something to eat. I think it's best from now on that they don't come to me. It just isn't working out, so instead I've arranged for my daily, Mrs Davies, to come here and look after them, but it can only be a temporary arrangement,' she warned him.

Watching her drive off, Lyle stuck bunched hands into his trouser pockets. Damn her for her interference! He scowled blackly, unaware of how much he looked like his recalcitrant sons. What kind of woman would advertise for a husband, for God's sake? But he supposed he would have to see her now, otherwise Justine would raise merry hell and he depended too much on his sister to risk antagonising her.

He turned away from the window and looked at the door. Now he would have to go upstairs and tackle the boys. Cravenly he found himself longing for a restorative whisky and soda before doing so, but he refused to give in to the urge.

Justine had been right about one thing. They *were* his children...his responsibility and one that he was not tackling very well at all. It was all very well to know in theory what to do, but in practice two sulky and silently condemning children seemed to be able to frazzle his nerves far faster than the most awkward patient

He found them in the room linking their bedrooms, which was designated as a study. Both of them were sitting down, so close together that their bodies were touching.

They looked more like him than Heather. They had his height and colouring, but their eyes were Heather's, deeply hazel, and now both of them gazed accusingly but mutely at him.

He sat down, feeling ill at ease and ill equipped to deal with them. What on earth had possessed them to play that stupid and dangerous game with their cousin? They were not unintelligent kids, far from it.

He took a deep breath.

'Okay...your Aunt Justine has told me all about this afternoon. What you were doing was very, very wrong, and very dangerous. Peter could have been seriously injured if you had set that bonfire alight, killed even.'

Two pairs of unblinking hazel eyes regarded him without expression. It was like talking to a brick wall. He knew that he was simply not getting through to them. Exasperated and exhausted, he pushed irate fingers through his hair. His hand itched to administer punishment of a more basic nature than a lecture, but Heather had been resolutely against any form of physical punishment and he had felt bound to abide by her wishes, even though he himself as a boy had felt his father's hand against his backside on more than one occasion—events

which he remembered without rancour when he recalled the misdeeds that had given rise to them.

'Your Aunt Justine can't look after you any
more.' He frowned, a solution presenting itself to
him, and added slowly. 'Perhaps I ought to send you
both away to school.'

Briefly both sets of hazel eyes mirrored fear, and
he had a momentary urge to reach out and enfold
them reassuringly, but he knew that any attempt on
his part to touch them would be fiercely repudiated.
He had already talked over with Justine the wisdom
of sending them away to school but she had been
vehemently against it. 'If you do they will grow up
institutionalised, Lyle,' she had told him. 'They
haven't got enough self-confidence in themselves for
that. They'd think of it as punishment.' And now
looking at them he could see that she was right.

'Okay, no boarding school.' He felt rather than
saw them relax, and wished a little despairingly that
they were not so close to the long school holiday.
Previously they had stayed with Justine during the
week, coming home to him at weekends, but today
she had made it plain that that could not continue.

Justine had forced him into a corner with marriage
as his only escape. But marriage was the last thing
he wanted. His marriage to Heather had been a living hell, and he had loved her. But this marriage
that Justine was promoting would not be like that,

it would be a business arrangement, like employing a housekeeper or a nanny.

'Why can't the pair of you make more of an effort to get on with Peter?' he demanded wearily as he got to his feet. 'Your Aunt Justine loves you, but...'

'No, she doesn't.' Stuart's lip curled as he spoke. 'She doesn't love us at all,' he continued, watching him. 'She just puts up with us because *you're* our father.'

There was enough truth in what he was saying for Lyle to be lost for a way to answer.

'No one loves us,' James piped up. 'And we don't love anyone, just each other.'

Slowly Lyle backed towards the door. Poor wretched little brats... But what on earth could he say to them? That he had loved the four and two-year-old sons he had been forced to leave when Heather wanted her divorce, but that the ten and twelve-year-olds they now were were strangers to him? Heather had demanded sole custody and had told him that she thought it would be better for the children if they didn't see him, and his solicitor had advised him to accept her demands, so they had come to him virtually strangers.

Justine was right, he thought, opening the door abruptly. They did need someone of their own. She was also right about the pressure of his personal problems and the effect it was likely to have on his work, and as a doctor he could not afford to make mistakes.

What was she like, this woman who advertised so boldly for a husband, merely describing herself as twenty-six, single and self-supporting?

Well, thanks to Justine it looked as though he might soon find out.

CHAPTER TWO

ONCE HAVING MADE UP her mind to find herself a
husband Jessica was amazed at how calm she felt
about the whole thing.

She did not anticipate that David would attempt
to tell Andrea what she was doing; to do so would
constitute far too hard a blow to his pride, and she
suspected that he found it very convenient to hide
his brief flings with his female students behind her
sister's neurotic belief that he was having an affair
with her.

More surprisingly however, neither did it stop him
from attempting to make headway with her himself.
She was a regular visitor to the university library,
and it irritated her how often he managed to waylay
her there, subjecting her to the heavy gallantry and
smug male egotism that she most loathed about him.

His skin was so thick nothing could dent it, she
reflected bitterly after one such encounter. He still
refused to believe that she would actually get married and constantly taunted her about it, to the extent
that she felt she would virtually marry the first man
who asked her simply to prove him wrong.

Over and above all this, Andrea's mental state worried her increasingly, and she was finding it almost impossible to concentrate on her work. She needed a calmer, more relaxing environment. She grimaced faintly to herself. Marriage, from what she had observed of it, was scarcely conducive to such virtues, and then because her sense of humour was highly developed and sometimes disconcertingly self-directed she wondered if embarking on such a marriage as she planned *would* confirm her research on arranged marriages, and how she would cope if it did not.

IF SHE HAD WONDERED what sort of person responded to advertisements in the personal columns, she was no nearer to discovering the answer over a week later when she had read through the replies she had received.

After discounting the cranks and frankly obscene responses she was left with over a dozen apparently genuine replies all from men who seemed united in only one thing—their loneliness. Apart from one, that was.

Thoughtfully she picked up the letter which had seemed so different from all the others and read it again. For one thing, it was much longer than the other replies; it was also extremely detailed and direct giving her much more information than her other correspondents, even to the point of being almost 'chatty' in places.

It described both the house and life-style of the writer, and made no bones about the problems he was experiencing with his two sons, nor his reasons for wanting a wife, 'Primarily to take care of the boys and give their lives a focal point, and secondarily to provide for myself a well-organised home life, so that I can concentrate on my patients.'

It contained no false promises of emotional commitment or mutual happiness, being rather severely practical. In short, it represented a subtle challenge and the ideal background against which she could test out her research behind her new book, and Jessica felt herself responding to that challenge, her response in no way lessened by the knowledge that the letter was carefully designed to elicit such a response.

She was surprised by the degree of sympathy she felt towards the two boys, described unflatteringly in the letter as 'a pair of holy terrors designed to try the patience of a saint, and who, despite their insecurities and needs, manage to be as obnoxious and unlovable as it is possible to be.' No false imagery there. It was the cry of an exasperated adult, exhausted by the emotional problems he was ill-equipped to solve.

She retained sufficient memories of her own parents' divorce to be fully aware of the nature of the children's problems, and going into such a household was hardly likely to leave her as much free time as she was used to, to concentrate on her work, but despite that she found herself reading and re-reading the letter. Absently she searched among her books for a map, and found that as he had guessed the village was less than seventy miles away. Far enough away to put a distance between her and David, but close enough for her to get back quickly if Andrea needed her. Rather oddly the letter named a day and a time for a prospective meeting, taking things forward faster than she had anticipated. She wasn't sure if she was ready for a direct confrontation with her prospective spouse as yet, but he it seemed had no qualms. The letter included a map and directions, she noticed, but no surname or telephone number so that it would be impossible for her to ring up and cancel the appointment. She simply either had to turn up or ignore the letter completely. Plainly there were not going to be any half measures.

How would she like being married to a doctor? Contrary to popular opinion she had found that they were often harassed, ill-mannered brutes, anxious only to empty their surgery, but she was quite willing to be proved wrong. She had nothing against the breed *per se*.

A sense of adventure, long dormant inside her, made her lips curl in a slow smile, a feeling of lightheartedness, so alien after the miseries of the past months that it felt like champagne in her veins, and impelled her to study her diary. If she had nothing on on the day stipulated in the letter than she would go, she decided rashly, unaware that she had been holding her breath like an excited child until she turned over the pages and found the date completely free of other engagements.

Telling herself that it was completely ridiculous to decide what could be the whole of her future on such a simple whim, it nevertheless pleased her to find the date free. Guiltily she acknowledged that she had been playing a silly game of pretending she was not responsible for her own fate, and that somehow it lay in other, more powerful hands, thus also avoiding taking any responsibility for what might happen. Sometimes it was decidedly uncomfortable being a psychologist, she decided wryly. There were odd occasions when she might have preferred to remain in ignorance of her own motives.

Admittedly it was a little disconcerting to realise that on Friday she was going to have to face a stranger who might ultimately end up as her husband—and Friday was only two days away, but what was there to be gained by delaying? Daily Andrea grew more demanding, more frighteningly hysterical and emotional.

The scarlet Mercedes 380SL which had been her one extravagance on the fruits of her commercial success made light of the seventy miles from her home to Sutton Parva. The car was a childish indulgence which she knew she ought to have resisted, but which one part of her was stubbornly glad she had not. For one thing, it was extremely impractical having only two full seats and a very small back one, for another it guzzled petrol. But on a sunny day like today, with the soft top down and the scents of the countryside, not to mention the exhausts of other vehicles, freely available to her, she was unable totally to banish the faint thrill of pride that owning the vehicle gave her.

Having found the village she drove out of it again and stopped the car on a quiet country road to study her instructions and the map more carefully.

She didn't want to be seen stopping in the village, where she would no doubt be remembered and perhaps gossiped about later, especially if... Illogically her mind shied away from the potential outcome of today's meeting, and it was while she was mentally taking herself to task for this that the impatient blare of a car-horn reached her. Frowning, she swivelled round in her seat to see a tall dark man bearing angrily down on her from the ancient estate-car, parked only yards behind her.

A face which might otherwise have been described as handsome was screwed up in an expression of furious impatience, overlong thick black hair brushing the collar of a cotton checked shirt.

'Sorry to interrupt Madam's daydream,' a harsh male voice gritted scornfully, 'but you're blocking the road, and have been for the last five minutes.'

Guiltily Jessica was aware of having been so engrossed in her own thoughts that she had been deaf to his arrival, but even so his impatient manner irritated her.

Coolly she let her eyes drift over his hard-boned face, noting the aggressive thrust of his jaw, and the dangerous flash of fire in his eyes.

He was breathing heavily, or rather almost snorting like an enraged bull, she thought in some amusement, noting the rapid rise and fall of his chest, and the strain his rage was putting on the four out of half a dozen or so buttons that enclosed it.

'Finished the inventory?'

The scorn in his voice should have embarrassed her, especially since she was not in the habit of staring so openly at any man, stranger or no. Lean hips tapered down to long legs, and aware that it was annoying him, she deliberately let her glance linger before saying demurely, 'Er…it seems that your zip's gone.'

There was a moment's stunned pause, compounded of astounded silence on his part and unholy glee on her own. She wasn't quite sure why, but it amused her intensely to see such an arrogantly male man so utterly confounded.

He looked down, swore briefly and then turned

his back on her, while she fought against the bubbles of laughter threatening to escape from her throat. By the look of him if she dared to laugh he was quite capable of murdering her.

When he turned back to her, he was still furiously angry although he was obviously trying to control it.

'My apologies,' he said between gritted teeth. Very nice white teeth, Jessica noticed absently. 'But I am in something of a rush, so if you could bring yourself to shift your car.'

A rush? Why? Had he been on the point of being discovered by some angry husband? She looked at him and saw two things reflected in his eyes. The first was that he had guessed what she was thinking and the second that he was absolutely furious about it.

Almost she was tempted to dither, just to see what effect it had on him, but wisdom persuaded her otherwise, and so neatly reversing the Mercedes right to the side of the road, she made room for him to pass, which he did crashing his gears awfully and sending up a cloud of dust, which descended on the Mercedes' immaculate paintwork in tiny gritty particles.

She spent another five minutes studying her map and then realised guiltily that she was going to be late for the appointment. Luckily she found the house on her first attempt, momentarily appalled by the uncontrolled wilderness that passed as a garden, as she drove slowly up the drive and parked outside the front door. The drive continued round the side of the house and presumably to the back, but Jessica had no intention of trusting her precious car to the gaping holes she could see in the fragmented drive that lay beyond the front door.

She climbed out of the car without bothering to look in her mirror. Her hair was slightly tangled from the drive, and she had put make-up on before setting out, but apart from that she had made no other feminine concessions to what lay ahead. After all if this man wanted to marry her it would be for reasons other than her looks. Indeed it would have to be because one thing she intended to make very clear indeed was that this would be a marriage in name only.

A noticed pinned to the front door announced that the waiting room and surgery lay to the left of the door, and that all other callers were to press the bell.

Dutifully she did as instructed, and had to wait so long for her summons to be answered that she turned her back on the front door and instead surveyed the wild tangle of rhododendrons that lined the drive-way, some of them dead, allowing a glimpse at the awesomely neglected lawns that lay beyond. It would take an army of devoted gardeners armed with scythes to cut down that lot, Jessica thought drily, looking in vain for the point where the lawn

ended and what she imaged must be the herbaceous
border began. Lupins gone frantically to seed and
almost uniformly blue were the only flower she
could actually recognise and she shuddered faintly
when she contrasted the overgrown wilderness in
front of her with the neatly ordered gardens surrounding her flat.

'Yes?'

The harsh voice was uncomfortably familiar and
decidedly unwelcoming, the shock in the blue eyes
as she turned to face him hardly flattering.

'God, it's you!'

Shock gave way to amusement as she recognised
the man who had accosted her so angrily earlier.

'I suppose you'd better come in then.'

He was scowling horribly at her, close to, even
taller than she had first thought.

She followed him inside, grimacing faintly to herself at the decidedly unfriendly grimness in his voice
as he pushed open a door and said curtly, 'In here.'

The room was a hodge-podge of unmatching furniture, most of it worthy only of firewood or a jum-
ble sale from what she could see. Closing her eyes,
Jessica tried not to think of her own carefully chosen
decor and antiques.

'So, you're looking for a man.'

The openly derisory tone of his voice caused her
eyes to narrow faintly. This antipathy was not what
she had expected from his letter.

'Oh no,' she responded blandly, hiding her smile as he looked warily at her. 'I can quite easily find a *man,*' she told him truthfully. 'What I'm looking for is a *husband,* and moreover one who is prepared to accept the restrictions I should want to place on such a relationship.'

If she had expected to provoke an adverse reaction by her provocative statement she would have been disappointed, Jessica admitted, watching him study her with the same thoroughness with which she had herself studied him so recently, although there was considerably less amusement in his eyes than there had been in hers, only a hard resentment which she recognised and wondered at. It was almost as though he didn't want to marry her—her or anyone else—she acknowledged, as though in some way he was being forced. She frowned and looked at him, watching his eyes narrow as they saw the comprehension in hers.

'That's right,' he said flatly. 'None of this is my idea, it's my sister's. She's the one who wrote to you, who brought you down here on this mad goose-chase.'

'I see.' Jessica studied him thoughtfully, half shocked by the swimming sense of let-down she was feeling. Good heavens, the man was rude, hostile and as patently the wrong type of material for the sort of marriage she wanted as it was possible for anyone to be, and yet she was feeling disappointed

because he was making it so plain that he did not
want her, or anyone else, as a wife.

Smiling calmly at him she made for the door.
'Then there's really nothing more to be said, is
there?' she said as she opened it.

'Wait a minute.'

She herself was tall, but she had to look up to
meet his eyes, half surprised by the strength in those
lean hands as he pushed the door closed.

As he leaned over her she could smell the faint
male tang of his sweat, and unconsciously she
shifted her weight so that she could move back from
it. She disliked the evidence of such male sexuality,
and even more she disliked the fact that she should
be aware of it, backing away as nervously as a
highly strung horse.

'What the devil?'

She watched his eyebrows draw together in a
frown, his mouth indenting with irritation.

'I wasn't going to touch you.'

He said it in a way that left her in no doubt of
his distaste of such an action, and irrationally his
vehemence stung. Was she so unattractive then that
a stranger was repelled by her?

'Why are you looking for a husband?'

The abruptness of his question when she thought
they had nothing left to say to one another made her
stammer slightly and hesitate before replying, but
she had nothing to hide, no reason not to tell him

the truth, so she did so, briefly explaining her concern over her sister's mental and physical state, as well as lightly touching on David's irritating manner towards her, but not at this stage mentioning her book.

'So, it's for your sister's sake, rather than any desire to get married, then, is it?'

Scorn touched her eyes shadowing them to dark gold. 'I would hardly marry for any other reason,' she told him bluntly. 'Marriage in my view is a form of self-inflicted torment, which these days is no longer necessary. In the past the only reason women have needed to marry is that they haven't had the freedom or the financial strength to make any other decision. Now it's being proved that a woman doesn't need a man to support her or her children. Why should she tie herself down in a relationship that almost always loads the dice in the man's favour?'

His eyebrows shot up, his mouth hardening even further as he demanded harshly, 'But what about those children, don't they have the right to have two parents to care for them?'

Refusing to let herself get annoyed, Jessica took her time in replying. 'Where they've been born into a marriage, yes, I agree that *those* children do need the support and care of both parents, but where a woman has elected to bear and raise her child on her own, then no.'

'You're aware that I have two children?'

He was still frowning and she said quietly, 'Yes.'

'And despite all you've just said you'd still be prepared to marry a man who had two dependent children—children moreover who are in need of considerable emotional support and attention?'

'I'm the child of a broken marriage myself,' Jessica told him slowly. 'I'm also a trained psychologist.' At any other time the amazement in his eyes would have amused her, but now she merely added, 'I have already written two books on the various aspects of human relationships, and at present I'm working on a third. Initially when I read your...that is your sister's letter, it struck me that I might be able to help your children.'

'Very noble of you.' He was practically sneering at her and suddenly she lost her temper, and said fiercely, 'Look, I can see I'm wasting my time even trying to talk to you. I've explained to you why I want to get married, and I'll go further and tell you that any marriage I do contract will not be with a man labouring under the burden of resentment and bitterness that you're obviously carrying. What I want is a civilised relationship with someone who accepts marriage as a business arrangement from which both parties derive certain benefits and forgo certain others.'

'Oh, really? And what would be the benefits you would be willing to forgo? Sharing your body with a lover because you'd have a husband to share it with instead?'

His tone was so deeply derisory that it was seconds before she could speak. When she did an angry flush lay across her cheekbones, her eyes deeply gold.

'Certainly not,' she told him crisply. 'I have no lover, nor would I expect to find one in my husband. Far from it.' She broke off, conscious that she had said too much, but to her surprise instead of taunting her further he was looking at her thoughtfully.

'I see.'

Quite what he did see, Jessica did not know.

'So you're talking about a platonic marriage, then, one which presumably could be set aside by mutual arrangement when it was no longer viable.'

'Yes, that's exactly what I had in mind,' she agreed stiffly.

'You realise that in my case, or rather in my sons', it could be several years before any such marriage could be dissolved.'

She did, and that was something which had worried her considerably initially.

'Yes, but provided you were prepared to allow me to continue with my career unhindered, our lives running side by side but separately, I would be quite willing to continue with the relationship for as long as was needful.'

'That could be for quite a long time. You're

young, only twenty-six. What happens if you fall in love?'

He was watching her very carefully now and Jessica knew that much hung on her response to this question. It was ridiculous that she should have this strange desire to convince him that she was a suitable candidate for the position as his wife, but she refused to dwell on her feelings, merely saying coolly. 'That will never happen. You see...' she let her eyes meet his, gold tangling with blue, 'I do not happen to believe in "falling in love". It's a euphemism, used at best to describe the emotional side of a strong physical desire for someone, and at worst as a crutch for the self-deluded.'

He looked at her for a long time and then said softly, 'Tell me, have you ever had a lover?'

Jessica didn't hesitate, knowing that she must convince him that it was not from any virginal fear of sex that she shrank from the commitment of marriage. Quite truthfully, she told him that she had and watched the way he controlled his reaction to her response, without adding that she had found it a singularly uninspiring experience and one which she had not bothered to repeat once that frail relationship had fizzled out, unable to survive the strain of their mutual disappointment in the physical expression of their desire.

Since then she had found it quite easy to rebuff any men who approached her sexually and privately she considered herself to be possessed of a rather low sex-drive, but that was not something she was going to impart to him. For one thing it was something it was not necessary for him to know, and for another... Mentally she dwelt on the sheer masculinity of the length and breadth of him and acknowledged that unlike hers, his physical experience was probably both vast and pleasurable.

It came as something of a shock therefore to hear him saying equably, 'Well, I hope you don't expect to find another in me. The one thing I *don't* want from marriage is sex.'

It was obvious from the way he was looking at her that she had not managed to conceal her astonishment as well as she had thought.

'And no, I don't have a lover,' he added harshly, 'and neither do I want one. To put it bluntly, the effects of my wife's death are such that I doubt if emotionally I am capable of making love. Well,' he challenged, in the silence that had fallen, 'do you still feel you want to marry me?'

'Yes, provided I can get on with the children.' How deeply he must have loved his wife! She was surprised to discover how unacceptable she found that knowledge.

It was not the answer she had intended to give at all, and she could hardly understand why she had given it. Plainly he was equally astonished. To cover up her own inner shock she added crisply, 'Your sexual prowess or lack of it is of no interest to me. All I want from you is...'

'The protection of my name as your husband. Yes, yes, you've already told me that.'

He really was the most exasperating, rude man. Jessica fumed on the point of whirling round and walking out on him, when they both heard the sound of a car outside.

She watched him stride over to the window, his lean body moving with a totally unexpected grace.

'My sister,' he told Jessica flatly. 'She's got the boys with her. Do you want to stay and meet them?'

Tacit acceptance of the role she might be going to play in their lives? Jessica didn't know, but suddenly she no longer wanted to leave.

'Too late, they're on their way in.'

The door opened to admit a tall dark woman with strained blue eyes which brightened immediately she saw Jessica, although she was careful to pretend that she had no idea who she was or what she was doing here, Jessica noted, watching her.

'You can stop the theatricals, Justine,' the hard flat male voice instructed. 'She knows it was all your idea.'

'Honestly, Lyle.' Impatience edged up under the wryly affectionate response.

So his name was Lyle. Unusual, but she quite liked it.

'I'd better introduce myself. I'm Justine Wheeler, Lyle's sister.'

'And matchmaker *extraordinaire*,' Lyle supplemented drily, breaking off as he realised the two boys were watching sullenly from the doorway.

'Come on in, you two.'

Turning to watch them Jessica recognised in their faces all the resentment and misery that had dogged her own teenage years. How well she could remember how fear and pain was blocked out with defiance and silence.

'Stuart, James, say hello to…'

'Jessica,' Jessica supplied for Justine, as she made the introductions. She made no attempt to touch or talk to the boys, but subtly let them know that she was aware of their presence, including them in her comments to Justine about her journey and the state of Lyle's garden.

It was acutely painful to watch their cautious approach to her. They were so frightened of being hurt that they instinctively recoiled from anything they themselves did not originate.

It was the elder one who spoke to her first, Stuart. 'Is that your car?' he demanded to know in a tone almost as truculent as that of his father, and watching the frown creasing the latter's forehead Jessica had to fight against an absurd desire to protect the child from his father's wrath.

'Yes, it is, do you like it?'

She watched him nod his head, and then told him that she had only recently bought it. 'The only thing is I can't manage to fathom out the seat-adjustment mechanism.'

She aimed the comment at the gathering in general, holding her breath until Stuart said offhandedly, 'I could try and work it for you.'

'Could you?' She accepted his offer as casually as he had made it. 'Okay, then.'

She didn't even look as both of them darted out of the room, and she certainly didn't turn round to see what they were doing when she heard the car door open, but she was standing in front of a mirror which gave her a pretty clear view of the interior of her precious car—and what was going on inside it.

'That was pretty clever,' Justine admired. 'You seem to have the right touch.'

'She ought to have. She's a damned psychologist,' Lyle muttered, giving his sister a look which seemed to say, 'Now look what you've landed me with.'

'The boys will be back shortly,' Jessica interrupted calmly. 'I can tell you now that I'm prepared to marry you with the provisos we've already discussed. The rest is up to you. I'll leave it to you to get in touch with me if you feel you want to take this any further.' She handed him one of her cards, and composed her face into an appreciative smile as both children trooped back in and Stuart loftily announced that it was quite simple to move the seat, and that he would show her how before she left.

CHAPTER THREE

BY WEDNESDAY of the following week Jessica had convinced herself that she was not going to hear from Lyle, and what was more she couldn't understand why she should even want to. He was the most difficult, unappealing man she had ever come across, and marriage to him would be no sinecure. Which made it all the more startling when he did ring late on Thursday evening, that she should feel such a thrill of excitement at hearing his voice, less truculent than she remembered but still slightly abrasive, as he told her that having thought over everything he would like to go ahead with their marriage, provided she was still agreeable.

She was tempted to prevaricate and make him wait, but only that morning she had had another hysterical telephone call from Andrea and so instead she said calmly that she was.

'Fine, that only leaves us to organise dates. As far as I'm concerned the sooner it's done the better. School holidays start next week, and I'll need you here to take charge of the kids.'

Stifling half-hysterical laughter, Jessica agreed calmly that she could see the necessity for haste.

'I'll make all the arrangements and then get in touch with you. Are there any dates you specifically want me to avoid?'

Having checked her diary and confirmed that there were not, Jessica thanked him politely for his call and said goodbye. It was like living in a dream, she reflected when she had done so; and hardly seemed at all real. It was impossible to believe that by this time next week she might actually be married. But that was what she had agreed to do, and she had her own arrangements to make. She would have to find a tenant for her flat; but that would not be a problem, she knew. And then there was her work...

By Sunday she had done everything there was to do. In the morning Lyle rang, his voice flat and emotionless as he told her that he had arranged the ceremony for two o'clock on Monday afternoon.

That meant she would have to tell Andrea today, Jessica reflected when she had replaced the receiver.

Not quite sure how well she would be able to carry off the role of bride-to-be in her sister's presence, she took the cowardly way out and telephoned her.

The spate of questions that followed her bald announcement finally culminated in a stunned, 'Married? You? I can hardly believe it, Jess. Why?'

She could have said, because you told me it was the only way you would accept that I'm not having an affair with your husband, but somehow she managed to restrain herself, and said instead, 'Oh, for all the usual reasons.'

'But you've not said a word...'

'Well, there wasn't much point. We've only just made up our minds.'

'I suppose you met him when you were doing the research for your book,' Andrea commented. 'But really, you might have told me, I am your sister, your closest living relative since Mum and Dad divorced.'

'I couldn't say anything because I wasn't sure how...how serious Lyle was. He has two children from his first marriage and...'

'He was worried about them accepting you, I suppose. God, Jess, I can't imagine you with a couple of stepsons. How old are they?'

Jessica obligingly told her, adding as casually as she could that since the school holidays were about to start she and Lyle had decided to get married as quickly and as quietly as they could.

'When?' Andrea demanded.

Taking a deep breath Jessica told her.

'Tomorrow? Are you serious?'

By the time she had managed to convince her sister that she *was* serious, and that she was not out of her mind, Jessica was feeling limply exhausted.

She was also beginning to wonder if she were not additionally slightly crazy. Surely there had to be an easier way to convince her sister that she wasn't the remotest bit interested in her husband? But even as the thought formed, she had a mental picture of two solemn little faces watching her drive away, two pairs of hazel eyes regarding her departure with a stoicism and an indifference that she well remembered from her own childhood. They were so vulnerable, they needed her. What child wouldn't with a father like theirs? Aggressive, domineering, totally incapable, or so it seemed, of understanding his children's pain.

No doubt he had never really wanted them. She could still remember her own pain when she realised that her father loved his girlfriend more than he loved Andrea and herself.

She deliberately kept herself busy for the rest of the day, filling boxes and cases with her belongings, exhausting herself to the point where by nine o'clock all she wanted to do was have a bath and crawl into bed. When the doorbell went her heart leaped like a stranded fish, her pulse-rate increasing threateningly, until she opened the door and discovered Justine standing there.

Why on earth had she thought her caller might be Lyle? And why was she so disappointed that it was not?

'Sorry to barge in on you like this,' Justine apologised, following her inside, 'but I thought I'd come and have a chat with you without Lyle around.'

'Umm, this is lovely.' She made a face as she glanced round Jessica's small sitting-room. 'Lyle doesn't seem to have the faintest idea about décor. You'll have to take him in hand there. Despite the shabby furnishings and that awful car, he isn't a poor man by any means.'

'I'm not marrying him for financial reasons,' Jessica told her calmly.

'No, I know. He's told me all about your sister and her husband.' She smiled rather uncertainly at Jessica. 'I hope you don't mind, but I wouldn't give him any peace until he told me.'

'Just like you didn't until he agreed to see me,' Jessica suggested calmly.

Justine had the grace to blush. 'I know it seems very high-handed of me, but you have to understand that I've been at my wits' end, especially where the boys are concerned. They don't like me, and I must confess after what they tried to do to Peter, I'm not too keen on them, but I do feel sorry for them, poor little scraps.'

'Yes, it can't be very pleasant, knowing that your father doesn't want you,' Jessica agreed drily.

'What?' Justine had been staring out of the window and now she spun round, her eyes widening. She really was ridiculously like her brother as far as looks went, Jessica thought absently, but fortunately she lacked his hard, cutting edge. 'Where on earth did you get that idea?' she demanded indignantly, causing Jessica to revise her opinion slightly. 'Lyle adores them both. It's just that they can't or won't respond to him. It tore him apart when he and Heather divorced and she demanded that he give up all his rights to them. Heather was the one who didn't want children, she didn't even want to marry Lyle in the first place. When she found she was pregnant she was furious; she wanted to get an abortion, but Lyle refused to help her and insisted instead that they got married.' She sighed and added, 'I know he must seem a terrible grouch, but like all intelligent men who can't bear to admit that their intelligence wasn't enough to prevent them from the folly of falling in love with the wrong person, he's now determined to treat our sex with the utmost suspicion. It would break my heart if I let it. Sometimes I can hardly believe how much he's changed.' She shook her head sadly. 'And of course he still blames himself for Heather's death.' She saw Jessica's expression and explained quickly what had happened to her sister-in-law.

'The plain truth is that Heather was a spoilt, temperamental little bitch who never put anyone ahead of herself. It's no wonder those poor kids are so screwed up. They must be so scared inside.'

'Yes, that's what I thought.'

The two women exchanged a long look.

'You do mean to marry him, then?' Justine said at length.

'I've said that I will.'

'He's told you I take it that the marriage will...'

'Exclude sex?' Jessica said for her. 'Oh, yes, we've been into all that. Quite frankly, if that hadn't been the case I wouldn't have agreed to marry him. I seem to be one of those women who have an extremely low sex drive,' she added in answer to Justine's unspoken question.

'Well, I wish you luck with what you're taking on,' Justine told her frankly. 'And if I can do anything to help—'

She liked her prospective sister-in-law, Jessica reflected, when Justine had left. There were the makings of what could be a rapport between them already. Justine had explained to her that her husband worked abroad for one of the oil companies, but that she was expecting him home in the near future.

'You'll have your hands full with Stuart and James,' she had warned just before she drove way, and Jessica had smiled rather grimly, privately reflecting that it was not the two boys that were going to cause her the most trouble, but their irritatingly masculine father. It struck her later as she prepared for bed that it would have made life much easier for her if Lyle were less physically attractive. Days later she was still vividly aware of the maleness of him—

aware of it and faintly disturbed by it, without really being able to analyse why.

THEY WERE GETTING MARRIED at two o'clock in the afternoon and the arrangements were that they would meet at the register office and then after the ceremony drive separately to Sutton Parva where Jessica would unload the first of her possessions from her car, transporting the remainder of them to her new home over the next week.

By twelve o'clock she was more nervous than she had ever been in her life before and totally convinced that she must have been mad even to think of entering into such a commitment.

At twelve-fifteen the phone rang and she cravenly hoped it might be Lyle saying that the wedding was off. But it wasn't, it was Andrea, ringing primarily to wish her 'good luck', and to check that she had not had second thoughts about not wanting her to attend the wedding.

Once she had confirmed this Andrea said guiltily, 'Jess, I feel awful about those things I said to you, but I was so frightened I was going to lose David to you. You're everything I'm not. Clever, successful... David's got a real thing about you. He never stops comparing us. I'm so relieved that you're getting married! I'm sure that once he accepts that you're out of his reach, he'll turn back to me again.'

And Jessica knew that there was no escape left for her. She would have to marry Lyle.

At one-thirty, just as she was about to go out to her car, a taxi drew up outside and as she watched, Lyle got out. He looked unfamiliar in his dark formal suit and crisp white shirt, and for some reason as he turned to look up at her window, her heart lurched drunkenly. What was he doing here? Her palms were sweating slightly as she opened the door to him. He looked at her in silence for a moment, slowly taking in her cream linen suit and high-heeled shoes.

'I thought I'd come and collect you,' he told her by way of explanation. 'I didn't want you getting cold feet.'

For a moment their eyes met, and Jessica knew that he shared every one of her doubts, but that like her he was determined to go through with the marriage.

All the way to the register office she tried to tell herself that she was doing no more than millions of women before her had done; reminding herself of how in her book she had praised the institution of arranged marriages.

Lyle was driving. She had been too bemused to beat him to the driver's seat, and unexpectedly after that brief demonstration she had had of his ability he was proving to be a good driver.

The register office was surprisingly festive, decorated with fresh flowers, the registrar a charming man in his mid-forties, who greeted them with a smile.

The service was brief, but not rushed, and it was only after it was over that she realised the enormity of what she had done. It was like being douched with cold water. She turned automatically to Lyle to tell him that she had made a mistake, and totally unexpectedly he smiled at her; really smiled for the first time. The world spun dizzily round her, her lungs bursting as she forgot to breathe. It was like suddenly discovering a totally unexpected and powerful ally in the middle of an alien and terrifying war, and its effect on her was so paralysing she could do no more than stare at him open-mouthed.

'Jessica?'

The smile was gone, his eyes sharply questioning, the impatient sound of his voice bringing her back to reality.

'I've left the boys with Mrs Hedges, my receptionist-cum-nurse. She won't be pleased if we're late back.' He looked rather grim and she suppressed a faint sigh.

'Do they know about...that we're getting married?' she supplemented, still unwilling to use the word 'us' in connection with them as a unit. She had a feeling that Lyle had no desire to be thought of as part of a married couple. He had married her to provide his children with a substitute mother, not because he wanted a wife.

'I told them last week, after you'd agreed,' he informed her, maddeningly not adding anything else.

How had they taken it, Jessica wondered. Had they been shocked, hurt, surprised? Well, she would be able to find out for herself soon enough.

Lyle had parked his car quite close to the register office and while she got into her own he went off to get his.

She didn't feel married despite the service, Jessica decided as they drove towards Sutton Parva. In fact she didn't feel any different at all, merely slightly disorientated. She didn't want to think too deeply about that illuminating moment in the register office when Lyle had smiled at her. It provoked too many questions she had no wish to answer.

Mrs Hedges, Lyle's receptionist, turned out to be a smartly dressed, well-upholstered woman in her mid-fifties, with carefully sculptured blue-rinsed grey hair. She looked, Jessica thought, as she was introduced to her, the type of woman who would be a staunch supporter of the local Women's Institute, and a demon for efficiency and routine.

She didn't express either surprise or curiosity when Lyle introduced Jessica as his wife, merely greeting her with a formal smile and explaining that she had to rush off as it was her bridge evening.

The two boys had followed her into the hallway and now stood side by side watching Jessica in silence.

There was something nerve-racking about such silent scrutiny, she acknowledged, forcing herself not to fill the void with empty chatter, sensing that it would be best to let the children come to her when they were ready.

She proffered them a smile and then turned to Lyle without speaking to them.

'If you'll show me my room, I'll make a start on emptying the car.' She paused and added uncertainly, 'I'll also need a room to work in if that's possible.'

'The house has six bedrooms,' Lyle told her, 'I've put you in one with a small boxroom off it which I had thought of converting into a bathroom, but somehow I've never been able to get round to it. If that isn't large enough for you to work in, then we'll have to find something else, although we're a little short on space downstairs because two rooms are taken up by my surgery and the waiting-room.'

'Isn't that a little old-fashioned?' Jessica commented as she followed him upstairs. 'I mean most places these days have modern purpose-built health centres, surely?'

'In the cities, and in commuter areas rich enough

to afford such luxuries, but not in the country.' He sounded rather grim.

'But what happens in case of an emergency, or if you're out on call?' Jessica persisted. She wasn't too happy at the thought of an emergency call coming through to the house when Lyle wasn't available.

'They have to call out the ambulance service from the cottage hospital. Between us we cover a radius of just over fifty miles. Not very reassuring if you happen to live on the outer edge of that radius and you need treatment urgently. I've been pressing the local health authority for funds to equip a small clinic here. There's room in the grounds to build a purpose-built unit, but it's the policy these days to cut down on facilities—not extend them.'

From his voice Jessica could sense the frustration he obviously felt, and it altered her view of him fractionally, giving her an insight into what she had previously thought of as merely bad temper, but which now she could see could well be a mixture of exhaustion, worry and frustration.

'This way.'

They were on a long, rectangular landing with several doors going off it. The floor was uncarpeted, the boards dull and in need of a good polish. House-work wasn't one of Jessica's favourite activities, but the boarding-school which both she and Andrea had attended after their parents' divorce had held old-fashioned views on cleanliness. Did Lyle have any help in the house? Surely he must, but from what she had seen so far it was of a very indifferent quality. It struck her as he strode across the landing and pushed open one of the doors how little she knew about him, or his lifestyle—which was now going to be *her* lifestyle. Dismayed, she followed him into the room. It was comfortably large, but furnished with the same poor-quality oddments as the rooms she had seen downstairs. An old-fashioned square carpet of indeterminate colour covered most of the floor, apart from the edges which to her horrified disbelief were covered in a cracked, grainy lino, which she vaguely remembered last having seen in her grandparents' house as a child.

'Not exactly the Ritz, I know.'

His voice had gone hard and faintly hostile and when Jessica looked at him he was regarding her with narrowed eyes, densely blue between their thick black lashes. Something inside her turned to warm liquid, a sensation so disturbing that she actually felt quite weak. It took her several seconds to conquer it and say calmly, 'I hope you won't have any objection to my making some changes in the house—at my own expense, of course.'

His eyes hardened, and she recognised that she had made a mistake. 'I bought the house complete with furniture from the previous occupant. He'd lived here all his life, and for the last part of it, completely alone. You can do what you want as regards decorating and refurnishing—but I'll pay the bills.'

Thus effectively stopping her doing anything more than the basic necessities, Jessica thought angrily. Since she left university she had been financially independent, and it galled her that he should dare to patronise her in such a way. She opened her mouth to tell him as much, and then realised that she herself had possibly been equally patronising; her comment perhaps even a little high-handed, and undoubtedly offensive to such a male creature, and so she tempered what she had been about to say by suggesting calmly, 'Why don't we go halves? That way I won't feel guilty if I'm a little extravagant here and there.'

To her relief he nodded, and walked past her to push open another door.

'This is the boxroom I told you about. It has this connecting door with your room and another to the landing. It's only small, but...'

'But large enough for my needs,' Jessica confirmed, going to look into the room. Because he was leaning in the doorway she had to stand close to him, looking over the arm he had propped against the door frame into the room beyond, as she mentally sized it up for her desk and computer equipment.

On the drive home he had discarded his jacket and immediately she was conscious of the move-

ment of his muscles beneath his white shirt. Her
body stiffened slightly as she again became aware
of the masculine scent of his skin, and automatically
she took a step back. He looked at her and frowned,
opening his mouth to say something, and then closing it again as he looked over her shoulder and into
her bedroom.

Instinctively Jessica looked too, smothering her
surprise when she saw Stuart and James standing in
the open doorway.

'Are you going to live here now?'

The question was Stuart's, his tone belligerent,
but Jessica didn't let it put her off. Children who
had been through the traumas they had endured were
bound to be suspicious about any further changes in
their lives; they would want to know and had a right
to know how permanent, or otherwise, her presence
was likely to be.

'Yes, I am,' she told them quietly.

'Does that mean that we won't have to stay with
Peter any more?'

Now it was James's turn to question her, and she
allowed herself to relax enough to smile.

'That's right. Your father thought it would be better if you could stay here in your own home, but
since he has to go out to work, he married me so
that I could stay here and look after you.'

She had given the problem of the two boys a great
deal of thought since agreeing to marry Lyle, and

she had promised herself that where possible she
would be as honest with them as she could be, so
that there could be no misunderstandings. Children
as suspicious and hurt as these two were needed the
reassurance of being told the truth.

'Will you go out to work?'

James again, his tone slightly more relaxed.

'I do work,' she told him, 'but I shall be working
here in this room.' She gestured to the small boxroom.

'So does that mean you'll always be here?'

Again that suspicion and doubt in Stuart's voice.

'Most of the time,' she told him. 'Sometimes I
might have to go away on business, but not a lot,
and I shan't be doing any work until after the school
holidays.' She regarded them quietly and then took
a deep breath; they were old enough to be curious
about adult relationships and she wanted them to
know right from the start that she was here on their
side, as someone who cared and not a gaoler.

'The four of us are a family now,' she told them,
'but it's going to be very strange for all of us at first,
because we're all going to have to get to know one
another and to find out if we can like each other,
and that takes time.'

'Does that mean you're going to be our mother?'
James asked.

Immediately Stuart's face closed up, his eyes bitter and mutinous. 'We don't want another mother,'

he told Jessica brutally, adding under his breath, 'mothers go away.'

Inwardly she wept for him, but she knew instinctively that now was not the time to give in to emotion.

'No, I'm not going to be your mother, James,' she replied answering his question and ignoring Stuart's comment, and then deliberately glancing at her watch she asked calmly, 'Did Mrs Hedges give you any tea? It's almost six o'clock now, so if she didn't, I think it's time we had some.'

It turned out that the receptionist had not made them a meal so Jessica went back downstairs letting Lyle guide her into the kitchen where she struggled hard to conceal her appalled distaste at its shabbiness.

This place wasn't a home, she thought, staring round at the shiny painted walls, dingy with dirt in places, noting the hideous 'fifties' cupboard which leaned drunkenly against one wall. She turned accusingly to Lyle, disturbed that he had not made more of an attempt to provide his sons with a more comfortable background—on his own admission he could afford it—but she managed to check back the words. There was no point in quarrelling with him at this stage. He had given her *carte blanche* with the place, and that would have to be enough.

Both the cupboards and the refrigerator were ill-stocked. Sensing her feelings, Lyle said offhandedly, 'Justine normally brings me some groceries when she brings the boys back on Fridays. Mrs Falmer who comes in once a week to clean takes care of the rest.'

Making a mental note to go shopping first thing in the morning Jessica decided that all she could give them to eat tonight was an omelette.

There was room to eat in the kitchen, which was a good size, but the Formica table she found folded against one wall was a leg short and could not be extended far enough to seat them all, so they had to eat in the dining-room which was at the back of the house, and as depressing as all the other rooms.

Tea was a silent meal, but she was pleased to see that both boys cleaned their plates. She had been worried that they might be faddy eaters, so emotionally disturbed that they had to be coaxed to eat.

When she saw that James was yawning over his milk, she decided that one of the first things she would have to do would be to talk to Lyle about their routine. Presumably during the week when they lived with Justine they had a set bedtime, but she was aware that this was an area where she would have to tread carefully before instituting any rules of her own.

When they had all finished eating Lyle excused himself, saying that he had some work to do. Taking this as a sign that he did not wish to be disturbed, Jessica took their dishes into the kitchen and washed up. Neither boy offered to help her, but both of them hovered round her while she was working, saying nothing, but watching everything she did. When she had finished she said calmly, 'Right, now I'm going to empty the car.'

Both of them followed her, Stuart in particular eyeing her Mercedes with distinct lust. Repressing a small smile, she started to take the first of her cases out of the boot.

She was halfway upstairs before she heard the noise behind her, and looking over her shoulder she saw that Stuart and James were coming behind her, carrying another case. It was a better start than she had hoped for, but she could not delude herself that there was not still an awfully long way to go.

It struck her then that the marriage which she had entered primarily for her sister's sake seemed to be taking on a different emphasis.

Wryly amused by the distinctly matriarchal vein she had discovered within herself, she wondered if the crusading instinct she had developed towards the boys sprang from genuine concern for them, or from her unhappy memories of her own childhood. Time alone would tell, and after all she had plenty of that now. This marriage she had entered into was a *fait accompli* and her deeply ingrained sense of responsibility towards Andrea now seemed to have extended to include her new husband's two sons.

CHAPTER FOUR

'JESS?'

She looked up from the patch of garden she had been weeding, brushing her hair back off her face.

'Over here, Stuart.'

It was nearly a month now since she and Lyle had married—a month during which her life had changed so much she herself found it difficult to comprehend how much at times. She often felt she was a completely different person from the Jessica who had calmly and logically sat down to find herself a husband in order to protect her elder sister, and to put her theories on marriage to the test.

As she heard Stuart coming up behind her, she turned to smile at him, ruefully noting the dusty patches on both knees of his jeans and the fact that somehow in four short weeks he seemed to have managed to grow a good two inches. Mentally adding yet another chore to an already long list, she sat back on her heels and waited to discover what he wanted.

'The decorators have arrived,' he announced importantly. 'They want to see you.'

'Okay, I'll come now.'

Her first priority as far as her new home was concerned, once she had been all through it, was complete redecoration throughout. She had spent almost a week making careful sketches of all the rooms and then putting together her ideas before she communicated them to Lyle.

He had studied her sketches in silence for several unnerving seconds and then quite unexpectedly he had asked, 'What about my room? You haven't included it here.'

A deliberate omission. Jessica was acutely aware of the fact that as far as Lyle was concerned, a wife was something he most definitely did not want, at least not on a personal basis, so she strove to keep out of his way as much as possible—not difficult, given the appallingly long hours he worked; and she had also refrained from doing anything that might be construed as an attempt to intrude on his privacy.

'I thought you might have your own ideas about what you wanted.'

'Not really, although I could do with better cupboard space.'

'I've got a firm coming out to measure for a new kitchen. All the bedrooms need proper wardrobes, I can get them to do a quote for your room too if you wish.'

Apparently he had wished, and he had also approved the drawings she had eventually shown him.

The local firm she contacted had been able to install the new fitments in the bedrooms almost immediately, although the kitchen renovations were going to take much longer. Jessica had specific ideas about what she wanted in the kitchen.

Stuart and James had been allowed to choose their own furniture and wallpaper. Rather to her surprise, Stuart had shown a distinct artistic flair, something she was determined to encourage.

Watching the elder of her two stepsons fall into step beside her as they made for the house, she marvelled at how well both boys had adapted to her presence. Already she could see definite signs of improvement in both of them, but more especially in James, which she suspected was only to be expected, as he was the younger of the two and had only been a baby when his parents separated.

'You've got dirt on your face,' Stuart informed her, squinting at her as they walked into the house. She tried to rub it off, forgetting she was still wearing her gardening gloves, and Stuart grinned. 'You're only making it worse, let me.'

Obediently she bent towards him, trying not to grimace when he produced a rather grimy handkerchief and carefully wiped the mud off her cheek. Initially the more aggressive and withdrawn of the pair, she could now see that Stuart was also the more sensitive. When he smiled at her, openly and warmly as he was doing now, she could almost feel the physical jerk on her heart-strings. This feeling she had for both boys, but especially for Stuart, was something that totally astounded her. She had never experienced a maternal twinge in her life before marrying Lyle, but something in his sons reached out and touched her in a way that she found totally unexpected, and which she could only put down to the fact that because of her own childhood she found it easy to relate to and understand their miseries.

With Lyle she found herself increasingly nervous and ill at ease, searching for polite small talk whenever they were alone together, but conversely when she was with the children she felt completely relaxed and at ease. In fact when she thought about it, she felt happier now than she had ever done before. Happy in a way she found hard to define, fulfilled almost, as though she had found a long-sought-after niche in life.

Unhappily the response the boys gave to her did not extend to include their father, Stuart in particular being almost openly hostile to Lyle. So far Jessica had not been able to discover the reason for this, but suspected that it must have something to do with his mother's death. She had not made any attempt to force their confidences, though, letting them talk to her in their own way making sure she was available to listen to them when they did want to talk.

The decorators were also from a local firm, and Jessica had already discussed at length with them her ideas for the house. She wanted the walls rag-rolled in softly toning pastel shades, to add light and warmth to the high-ceilinged rooms, and she had stipulated that the paint must have a washable finish, mindful of grubby fingers and determined that the house must also be a home.

To provide continuity she had decided on a heavy-duty plain wool carpet throughout, in a mid-bluey-grey colour impervious to the odd muddy footprint.

The kitchen and two old-fashioned bathrooms had been her main problem, but she had eventually de-cided on hand-made fitments for the kitchen which were to be sponged and ragged in a soft peach and cream and traditional white sanitary ware for the bathrooms, conscious of the fact that she was after all sharing the house with three males, who were not likely to be particularly impressed with pretty pastels.

The decorators simply wanted to see her to check on the work schedule before they started, and once this had been confirmed they were soon busy car-rying in ladders and paint pots.

'Where's James?' she asked Stuart. She had promised to visit her sister, and rather to her sur-prise, when asked both Stuart and James had vol-unteered to come with her.

'Upstairs getting changed.'

'Umm. I'd better do that myself. And we'd better

get you some new jeans, you're shooting up like a beanstalk. I think you're going to be even taller than your father.'

As always when Lyle's name was introduced into the conversation, Stuart looked sullen, but Jessica pretended not to notice, casually remarking that it was a shame that Lyle was too busy to come with them.

'I'm glad he's not coming,' Stuart told her. He was frowning fiercely, kicking up dust from the lawn.

'Don't you like your father, Stuart?' Jessica challenged gently, feeling that it was time for her to stop ignoring his obvious antipathy towards Lyle.

'He doesn't like us,' Stuart responded, scowling. 'He didn't want us, Mum told us that.'

'I think you're wrong about that, Stuart.' She said it gently but firmly. 'In fact I know that your father loves you both very much, because he told me so.'

'He's never got any time for us.'

Her heart went out to the thin, gangly boy and she stifled the impulse to take him in her arms.

'That's because he's so busy, Stuart. Being a doctor means that he always has to be available for sick people, you know that.'

Stuart was still looking unreceptive, and feeling that to press the issue could possibly do more harm than good, Jessica let the subject drop. It was true that Lyle was kept extremely busy with his practice, but it was also true that in the evenings he tended to spend what spare time he had in his office rather than in the sitting-room with the rest of them, and Jessica wasn't sure if that was because he actually had work to do or because he wanted to avoid being with her.

Andrea was in the garden when they arrived, relaxing in a comfortable chair with her feet up. She looked much healthier, her figure plumper and her face relaxed. She greeted Jessica with a hug and an affectionate kiss, her pregnancy now showing beneath her cool smock.

'William's gone to play with some friends,' she explained when Jessica asked after her nephew. 'And David's gone away on business for a few days.'

Jessica hoped her distaste didn't show. She was quite sure that it wasn't only business that took David away from his wife's side, but if Andrea was happy with the situation she was not going to risk upsetting her. Neither of them had referred to Andrea's state of mind prior to Jessica's marriage, but there was a marked change in Andrea's attitude towards her, Jessica noted thankfully.

They didn't stay long, and it was when they were driving home that Jessica realised how much the axis of her life had changed. Andrea, who for so long had been her sole concern, now seemed less important to her than the boys.

Both of them were suspiciously quiet on the way

back, which Jessica put down to being in strange surroundings, but later on when they were all sitting down for tea, she discovered that she had been wrong.

For once Lyle was home in time to eat with them. His presence at the table put a strain on Jessica which she was at a loss to understand. Whenever he was in the same room with her, she felt herself straining not to give him the impression that she had any personal interest in him, without being able to understand why she should feel this need.

'So what have you three been doing today?'

It was James who answered him.

'This afternoon we went to see Jessica's sister. She's going to have a baby,' he added thoughtfully, his eyes going from his father's face to Jessica's. 'Do all married people have babies?' he asked her curiously. Across the table Jessica's eyes met Lyle's, alight with an amusement that did strange things to her pulse-rate. Quelling her instinctive desire to smile back, she concentrated on James instead.

'Not all of them,' she told him truthfully.

'But will *you* have them?' he persisted, and catching sight of Stuart's shuttered face, Jessica immediately understood the reason for his silence on the journey home.

'No,' she told James firmly, but it was towards Stuart that she looked, watching his tension relax slightly, and feeling her heart wrench afresh. She too knew what it was to look on in anguish while her father produced a second and apparently more dearly loved family than the one he had abandoned.

It was after James and Stuart were in bed that she decided she ought to do some work. Often in the evenings she spent an hour or so sifting through her research and collating it ready to start writing, using the computer she had now had transferred from her flat and installed in her small study.

She was busily engrossed in this work when she heard her bedroom door open, and thinking it must be one of the children, she got up and walked to the communicating door.

Shock held her immobile as she saw Lyle walking towards her. He never came into her room, never sought her out at all for that matter.

'I'm sorry if I've disturbed you.'

How deep his voice was, sending tiny shivers of reaction quivering through her muscles. 'But I thought it was time we sat down together and had a talk.'

'Do you want me to come downstairs?' How polite and stilted she sounded, she thought furiously, like a schoolgirl being hauled before a teacher for a lecture.

'No, here's fine.' He sat down on her bed, leaving Jessica to take the chair.

'You seem to be getting on very well with the boys.'

'They are responding to me,' she agreed cautiously.

'Far more than they've ever responded to me.' He sounded grim, and for the first time she realised how painful it must be for him to see his sons turn away from him and go instead to a stranger.

'They're both wary of you,' she told him quietly. 'I think possibly they're frightened to trust you, because of the divorce.'

She saw the look in his eyes and wished she had not had to tell him that, but as she saw it it was the truth. 'Stuart told me this afternoon that he thought you didn't want them.' She saw he was about to speak and went on quickly. 'I told him that he was wrong, but it doesn't help that you have to spend so much time on the practice.'

'No, I realise that, but it wasn't really about the boys that I wanted to talk.'

He wasn't looking at her now but he was frowning, and suddenly she felt desperately cold, goosebumps chilling her skin. Was he going to tell her that it wasn't working out, that he wanted to end their marriage? The fear that raced through her at the thought was shockingly illuminating, but she refused to acknowledge the truth, telling herself that it was because of the boys that she wanted to stay.

'From my point of view this arrangement is working out extremely well—better than I'd dared hope. The boys have taken to you—that much is patently obvious, but what about you, Jessica? Tonight when James mentioned the children you might have, it struck me that from your point of view this marriage is a very bad bargain. I confess that when Justine first told me what she had done I was too blazingly angry to see past my own resentment of being forced into a marriage I didn't want, to give too much thought to your side of things. To give up the pleasure of a husband and children of her own, merely to ease the emotional trauma of a sister, is a lot to ask of any woman, but in particular one as young and attractive as you.'

Her muscles quivered as he raised his head and looked at her. Attractive, he had called her, but not in any way that made her feel that *he* thought she was attractive. It had been a completely detached observation.

'It also makes me wonder what has happened in your past to make you apparently content to accept a life without sex.'

Was he probing to see if she had been genuine? Did he suspect that she might desire him? Indignation and fear filled her in equal parts. Of course she didn't! It would be totally undignified and pointless to want a man who had already made it plain that he had no desire for her.

'I don't have anything to hide if that's what you're asking.' She made her voice light and careless. 'Sex had never been a motivating force in my life; I doubt it is in more than a handful of women's. Most of my sex put love ahead of merely physical satisfaction.'

'And you don't believe in love?'

'I don't believe that falling in love, and the consequent surge of desire it brings, is a good basis for marriage, no. Romantic love as we know it today is after all a fairly modern invention, while marriage... We've been through all this before,' she reminded him, 'but if you're no longer happy with our contract...'

She felt his concentration sharpen, her stomach lurching as he swung his eyes to focus on her face.

'Meaning what, exactly?' he demanded softly.

She had angered him, she could see it in the sudden tension hardening his bones. His expression reminded her of Stuart's when he felt most threatened, and momentarily she wanted to reach out and touch him, reassure him as she did the little boy, but she managed to push out the impulse and force herself to say calmly, 'If you feel the marriage isn't working, then you may want to bring it to an end.'

He was frowning now. 'Meaning that that's what *you* want?'

Exasperated, Jessica shook her head. 'No, it isn't. Look, you were the one who wanted to talk, I assure you that I'm quite content with the status quo.'

'You're content with a marriage that's no marriage; with a life that's completely celibate? Why, I wonder?'

Jessica didn't like having her emotions analysed like this, it gave her a feeling of losing control, or somehow being in danger.

'Probably because I have a very low sex drive,' she said flippantly, 'Some people do.'

'So they do,' he agreed softly. 'But there could of course be another reason. Marriage is a very convenient cloak behind which to hide an affair.'

Jessica felt herself go tense. Was he actually accusing *her* of having an affair? Anger speared through her. Did he honestly believe that she had lied to him? Looking at him squarely, she said, 'But I have already told you that I am not.'

'So you have.'

Without another word he got up and walked through the door, closing it behind him.

All desire to work had left her, inside she felt awash with conflicting emotions. Why had she been so anguished at the thought of him saying the marriage must end? Because she cared very deeply for the boys of course. It was a comforting explanation, but something still niggled at her. She couldn't help remembering how often when she had interviewed those couples whose marriages had been arranged by caring parents, both parties had confided that although they had come to the marriage as strangers, love had grown between them.

Was that what she was so afraid of? That she might grow to love Lyle as well as his sons? How ridiculous. Their marriage was a world away from the type of arranged marriages she had analysed.

TWO DAYS LATER Lyle announced that he had to go to a conference on drugs following the changes in Health Service prescriptions, and that it was likely that he would be away overnight. Any emergency patients during his absence were to be directed to the cottage hospital, and since a locum could not be spared to take his place there would be no normal surgery.

He left on the Wednesday morning, straight after breakfast. Wednesday was Jessica's day for taking the boys to the local sports centre fifteen miles away. It was well equipped, with squash courts, a swim-ming-pool and a variety of other facilities, and once a week they spent most of the day there.

On discovering that neither of them could swim particularly well, Jessica had instituted lessons for them both.

They always concluded the outing with a visit to McDonalds for hamburgers and thick sticky milk-shakes, which Jessica privately found nauseating, but which the children seemed to enjoy. She was gradually making small changes in their eating pat-terns, replacing tinned and frozen vegetables with fresh, and substituting wholemeal bread for white.

She had noticed that Lyle, who during the early days of their marriage seemed totally uninterested in food, now did full justice to the meals she provided. Cooking was something she enjoyed, preferring simple fresh foods to those smothered in heavy rich sauces, and she repressed a faint grimace as James demolished two of the revoltingly anaemic-looking soft rolls she had bought them to go with their hamburgers.

It bothered her that neither boy seemed to have any friends, and she was determined that once they went back to school she would encourage them to bring schoolfriends back home with them. The school they had attended in Oxford was now too far away but Lyle had discovered a very good private school locally which took day pupils. Both boys were clever, although in differing ways. James was fascinated by her computer, and she had privately resolved that for Christmas he must have one of his own, while Stuart was far more interested in his environment, and was also an avid reader. Stuart was the one who helped her in the garden; James the one who enjoyed watching her work on her computer.

They now had a firm of contract gardeners who came out once a week to mow the large lawns and generally keep the place tidy, although the flower-beds were so large that Jessica found she needed to spend some time each week herself weeding them. It was a task she found strangely pleasurable and she had even bought herself some books on gardening and was now ambitiously toying with the idea of a two-tone cottage-garden border for next year.

Family life appealed to her and had revealed to her a side of herself she had never previously suspected existed. She put it down to the fact that her teenage years had been so unhappy and often wondered if by trying to give the boys the security she herself had never known she was trying to rewrite her own past and thus obliterate its pain.

Although he didn't spend much time with them, she was acutely conscious of Lyle's absence when they returned home. All three of them were tired, and Jessica herself was in bed by half-past ten, glad to close her eyes and go to sleep.

In the early hours something woke her and she lay for several minutes sleepily disorientated, wondering what it was that had disturbed her. When no sound was forthcoming she tried to go back to sleep, but by now she was wide awake, and thirsty besides.

Not bothering to pull on a robe she pattered downstairs in her nightdress, the thin cotton cool against skin chilled by the night air.

As always she had left the landing light on. She had discovered quite early on that Stuart in particular was afflicted by nightmares and had a horror of the dark. The easiest solution she had found was to leave the landing light on and his door slightly open so that she could hear him if he called out. Yawning slightly she pushed open the kitchen door and came to an abrupt halt.

Lyle was standing in front of the hotplate, apparently waiting for a pan of milk to boil. He turned as he heard her, frowning slightly. Apart from the towel wrapped round his hips he was nude, his skin and hair damp.

'Something wrong?'

A curious weightlessness seemed to have descended upon her; an inability to drag her gaze away from his body. He was magnificently male, his body hard and muscled, shadowed across his chest with fine dark hair.

'Jessica?'

Somehow she managed to look up at him. 'I thought you weren't coming back tonight.'

'I changed my mind. The conference was over earlier than I anticipated. What are you doing downstairs? Don't you feel well?' His gaze sharpened and ridiculously she was acutely conscious of the thinness of her nightdress and the fact that the kitchen light was probably strong enough for him to see right through it.

What did it matter if he could? The female body was scarcely an unfamiliar mystery to him, and she already knew that he had absolutely no sexual interest in her.

'No, just thirsty,' she told him. 'Something woke me up.'

'Probably me running a shower. I'm sorry.'

She walked towards the sink, turning on the cold tap and letting the water run.

'I wanted to have a word with you about your computer.'

She swung round, watching him deftly pouring the milk into his mug.

He came towards her carrying the pan and instinctively she stepped back, hating herself for the way her muscles tightened beneath her skin as he came close. Why was it she always felt this need to keep a certain distance between them?

'Don't worry.' His voice was sardonic. 'I'm not about to invade your precious personal space.'

Her skin flushed as she realised he had seen her recoil. Rather shakily she asked him, 'What was it you wanted to know—about the computer, I mean?' She was desperately conscious that while she was conversing quite normally with him on the surface, at another, deeper, more primitive level she was acutely aware of him in a way that set off a thousand alarm bells ringing in her nerve-endings.

'Whether it could be adapted to help me with some of my paperwork. I was talking to a colleague who uses one.'

'I don't see why not. It's an advanced model and capable of taking a variety of software.' She forgot to be wary as her mind concentrated on what he was asking her, and as he stepped forward to put the pan

into the sink his arm touched her own. A frisson of
totally unfamiliar sensation shot through her, the almost silk-like brush of his skin against her own
causing an electric reaction that made her muscles
seize and her breath lock in her throat. She could
feel him looking at her, but there was no way she
could meet his eyes. To feel so vulnerable and afraid
was a new feeling for her, and one she knew she
did not like. Slowly backing away from him she said
formally, 'Perhaps we could discuss it in the morning.'

'Of course.'

She saw his shoulders shrug, half fascinated by
the play of flesh and muscles.

'You really don't like my sex, do you? Or is it
just me who affects you this way?'

She stiffened and stopped moving, her voice un-
steady as she lied, 'I don't know what you mean.'

'Like hell.' His arm shot out, his fingers curling
round her wrist, dragging her forwards with such
force that she couldn't withstand him. He brought
her to within inches of his body, refusing to slacken
his grip on her, his voice dry with irony as he said,
'You should see yourself, Jessica. You're frozen
with rejection, your body's practically screaming at
me to let you go, and you do that every time I come
anywhere near you. Oh, don't worry, I'm *going* to
let you go.'

When he released her, her whole body started to

shake and she stepped back from him immediately, at a loss to understand the dark anger glittering in his eyes. She couldn't endure another moment in the kitchen with him, and forgetting her thirst she turned and stumbled towards the door.

All the way up the stairs her heart thudded against the wall of her chest, her legs so weak that she could feel them tremble. She was as unable to explain her own reaction as she was to understand Lyle's response to it.

shock, and she stepped back from him immediately,
a faint, betraying tremor of pain... [illegible] in
her eyes. She couldn't endure another moment in the
[illegible] with him, and forgetting everything she... [illegible]
and stumbled... [illegible]

All... [illegible] ... admitted wryly
the wild absurdity of... her figure... [illegible] that she could

CHAPTER FIVE

LIKE THE WARNING implicit in a spasmodically aching tooth, her inability to be totally open and honest
with herself whenever she tried to rationalise her
reactions to Lyle continued to niggle at Jessica's
conscience. The tiny spurts of adrenalin that raced
through her veins whenever he came too close to
her urged flight rather than fight, caution rather than
confrontation, but what was there after all to confront him about?

Once his initial antipathy towards their marriage
had subsided, in so far as the terms of their contract
were concerned he was practically a model husband.
He had even explained to her that part of his original
irritation had sprung from the fact that at the time
Justine had delivered her ultimatum he had been
right in the middle of the hay-fever season, with all
its attendant extra work.

The hours he worked honestly appalled Jessica,
and she found herself getting illogically irate about
the unfairness of a system that demanded so much
from one man. Her tentative suggestion that she
might be able to help him to process his work on to

the computer he was thinking of buying, regretted the moment she had made it, had been surprisingly well received, and for the last ten days or so they had spent an hour or more together each evening after surgery, and once the boys were in bed, steadily working through his files.

Watching him surreptitiously to observe him, Jessica was caught off-guard by the degree to which her own perceptions of him had changed. The ill-mannered, arrogant man she had first come up against had virtually been superseded by the caring, hard-working, if sometimes understandably irritable human being she was discovering him to be.

As they worked together in his office, sometimes he would make a comment as he handed her a file.

'Mrs Meadows,' he said briefly handing her a particularly bulky folder. 'She's sixty-two years old and suffering from senile dementia. Her condition has grown progressively worse over the last four years, and there's very little we can do to help her. And there are thousands of people suffering from the same affliction.' He frowned and got up from his desk, going to stand in front of the window. Without looking at him, Jessica knew that his frown was deepening; that his concern for the plight of Mrs Meadows was genuine and went deep.

'And it isn't just Mrs Meadows herself who suffers; her complaint affects her whole family—or what's left of it,' he turned round, and grimaced

faintly. 'Mrs Meadows lives with her daughter because technically senile dementia is not a condition
that requires the patient to be hospitalised. However,
with her it has now reached the stage where she's
virtually bedridden, although no bed can be found
for her in either our local hospital or the old people's
home, so the burden of caring for Mrs Meadows
falls on her married daughter. And it is a burden.
Mrs Meadows requires twenty-four-hour-a-day
care—like a small child, she cannot be safely left.
Imagine the burden that places on her daughter. Because of it her marriage has broken up—her husband
simply could not endure life with a wife who was
constantly tied to someone else, never able to go out
with him or take part in any activities that meant
leaving her mother alone.

'They have three children, and the whole family
live in a rented three-bedroomed cottage. The eldest
girl has just left home—she's sixteen, still little
more than a child, but she says she won't live at
home any more. She's both resentful of her mother
because of the time she has to give to her grand-
mother, and frightened that as she gets older she too
will be pressed into the same caring role as her
mother. The most damnable thing of all is that because of the care she receives from her daughter,
Mrs Meadows could well live, physically at least,
for another twenty years.'

PENNY JORDAN   99

Jessica was horrified by what he was telling her.
'But surely the Social Services...'

'They do what they can, but they're already over-
stretched. If there were the money available Mrs
Meadows could go into private care, but there isn't.
It's a problem to which there's no answer, and Mrs
Meadows's daughter is only one of hundreds of
thousands of women all over this country who have
virtually had to give up any idea of living what the
rest of us consider to be a normal life, because of
the burden of looking after older relatives. In a hospital patients are bodies, symptoms and operations,
but as a GP...'

He shook his head without finishing what he had
been saying and went back to his desk to extract
another file.

'Mrs Meadway...'

THE WEATHER had suddenly turned hot; not a pleasant heat, but a muggy, threatening one, sultry with
storm warnings.

Jessica was out in the garden. She found the work
both therapeutic and relaxing. With both boys at
home she didn't have much time to work on her
book and had put it on one side. It was less than
two months since she and Lyle had married, and yet
strangely now she could not imagine any other life.

Andrea's pregnancy was advancing smoothly.
Her sister had driven over to see her the previous
week, and Jessica had been delighted to see how
much calmer she was. The boys too were benefiting

from her marriage. They turned to her more and more, and only this morning James had hugged her impulsively. She put down her trowel and sat back on her heels, remembering. She had been sorting out the washing and had shouted at him on discovering a rip in his new jeans. To her amazement, instead of being suitably penitent he had rushed over to her and hugged her fiercely, mumbling in explanation as he drew away, 'When you shout you sound like a real mother.'

A real mother... Was that what she was becoming? Certainly she was more emotionally involved with the boys than she had ever imagined possible. She derived pleasure from their company even when they exasperated her. The feeling she had for them was in no way mawkish or sentimental, but it was a form of love, she recognised, startled by the discovery. How quietly and compellingly it had crept up on her, this concern and involvement with their lives, creating a bond which she knew she would hate to see severed. Her feelings for them had added a new dimension to her life; before she had loved Andrea, but now her relationship with the boys had brought a...yes, a richness to her life...a certain inner tranquillity she had not experienced from her literary and financial successes.

So this then was love, this mutual need and sharing of experiences, this knowing that in addition to teaching the boys, she was herself learning from them. Suddenly it struck her how acutely shut out Lyle must feel. Although James did not share Stuart's resentment of their father, neither of them sought out Lyle's company in the way they sought out hers. And now that she knew him better she realised how bitter this must make him feel. He was a complex man, and one who did not reveal himself easily to others. It gave her a warm, pleasurable sense of euphoria to know that when they were working together he shared with her some of his most intimate feelings, opening barriers which she sensed had been carefully constructed to keep the world at bay.

The boys' mother must have hurt him very badly, she realised, and then tensed slightly, a warning impulse seizing her muscles, alerting her to some as yet hidden danger. Shaking off the feeling, she went back to work smiling slightly. She was being too defensive and protective, what was wrong with feeling compassion and concern for Lyle? He was after all her husband, the person with whom she had elected to share her life, and it made good sense for her to encourage anything within herself that made it easier for them to get along together. Children were very sensitive to bad atmospheres between adults. It would not help the boys if she and Lyle were constantly at loggerheads with one another.

She was still in the garden when Lyle came home. She stood up, feeling slightly self-conscious in her brief shorts and top as he came striding towards her, instead of making straight for the house. He looked tired and tense, his skin drawn tight over the bones of his face, and it struck her suddenly that he seemed to have lost weight. Too many rushed and skipped meals—he was so busy he never seemed to have time to sit down and eat properly with them. She couldn't remember a single meal since they had married that hadn't been interrupted by a telephone call or a caller.

Heat prickled disturbingly along her skin, the heavy, moist air pressing down on her body. She was aware of tiny beads of perspiration gathering between her breasts and on her forehead, and she pulled off one of her gardening gloves to push her hair back off her face.

'You've been busy.'

'I enjoy it. You look tired.'

She saw the surprise in his eyes and coloured hotly without knowing why. Surely it was not breaking the rules of their marriage for her to comment on his drawn appearance?

'Migraine,' he told her briefly, 'that's why I came back. I'm going upstairs to lie down. Any emergency calls will have to be referred to the cottage hospital. If I'm lucky I might just be in time to stave off an attack, if not...' He looked grim, his voice faintly harsh, and Jessica knew why.

Her mother had suffered from excruciating migraine attacks, some so severe that they had actually physically paralysed her. She would never forget the trauma of getting home from school one afternoon and finding her mother's car parked in the drive, with her mother inside it, totally unable to move a single muscle. The doctor had told her mother that she had been lucky to get home before the attack became severe, and even now Jessica shuddered to think of the potential danger had her mother been paralysed while actually behind the wheel of the car, although their doctor assured her that most sufferers normally had sufficient warning signs to be able to anticipate when a bad attack was likely to hit them.

Already she could see that the pupils of Lyle's eyes were tensely dilated, his bones showing almost white against his skin, and she made no attempt to detain him, waiting until he was inside before following him into the house. The boys were watching television, and she went into the sitting-room to warn them not to disturb their father.

Going back to the kitchen she hesitated before starting to make a pot of tea. Her mother had always found the drink relaxing and helpful when taking her medication. She had also found relief in having her neck and shoulder muscles massaged, Jessica remembered, and it had normally fallen to her to perform this task.

Instinct warned her that Lyle would not welcome her interference for a variety of reasons. He was after all an intensely private man, and one who would not welcome anyone seeing him at his most vulnerable. In that at least they were alike. She too loathed being fussed over, preferring to crawl off and be alone if ever she was feeling under the weather, and yet despite the warnings instinct flashed to her brain she still poured him a cup of tea and set off upstairs with it.

As she paused outside his door, half of her hoped that he had taken his medication and succumbed to the drugging effect of it already, and yet even though caution warned her against it, she still pushed open his door and went in.

The curtains were closed to block out the afternoon light, but although the room was dim, it was still light enough for her to see. The air inside the bedroom was thick and cloying; a legacy of the oppressive heat outside, and Jessica made a mental note to get her own lightweight fan.

She knew that differing atmospheric pressures could be one of the things that could trigger off a migraine attack, and she paused for a moment to weigh up the advantages of the coolness provided by the fan against the disturbance the sound of it would make, before going over to the bed.

As she approached it and looked down at Lyle's sprawled body her stomach lurched uncomfortably, thoroughly unnerving her. He was lying on his front, breathing heavily, his eyes closed, his eyelids vul-

nerably waxy in contrast to the thick darkness of his
lashes. She had never observed a man asleep so
closely before and it had the strangest effect on her,
a welling up inside her of sensations she was at a
loss to understand, other than that they were a combination of a strange yearning, tenderness, mingled
with the same compassion she felt for Stuart when
he was being his most stubbornly proud and difficult.

Lyle had discarded his shirt. It lay on the floor at
her feet, the waist of his jeans low on his hips, revealing that she had been right to think that he had
lost weight.

His skin was faintly olive, and he was, she saw,
sweating heavily. Not sure whether she felt glad or
sorry that he was asleep, she started to turn round.

'What is it?'

His voice, slurred and painfully exhausted, halted
her. She turned round and looked at him. His eyes
were still closed, the pallor of his face now replaced
by a heavy, feverish flush along his cheekbones.

'I brought you a cup of tea. My mother used to
suffer from migraine and she found it helped her
system to absorb her medication.'

The grunt he gave could have meant anything, but
it did not seem indicative of any desire to retain her
company, and she turned back to the door again.

'What else did she find helpful?'

The question surprised her. She looked at him and

found that this time his eyes were open, although so dark and hazed with pain that she actually felt something twist uncomfortably inside her in sympathy.

'She liked me to massage her neck and shoulders,' she told him absently, overwhelmed with guilt for having disturbed him. She should have listened to that first warning voice and left him in peace.

Again he grunted what she thought was a non-committal response, a strange, electrifying shock rippling through her as he demanded, 'Do you think it might work for me?'

Slowly picking her words, she looked at him. 'I suppose it depends whether your migraine is tension-induced or springs from some food or atmospheric intolerance.'

'The weather doesn't help, but primarily it's tension.' He moved restlessly, and closed his eyes. 'God, I feel as if my damn head's about to explode.'

His voice was a tiny thread of sound, and instinctively, without having to analyse what she was doing, Jessica reached out and placed her hand against the back of his neck.

The corded, tight muscles gave back their own story, and automatically she began to knead the taut constrictions, her fingers instinctively remembering the expertise she had learned with her mother.

Imperceptibly she felt him start to relax, his breathing slowing, easing. When she stopped and looked at him, without opening his eyes he muttered hazily, 'That feels good, don't stop.'

Slowly at first, and then with gathering confidence as she felt the tension slide out of his muscles, Jessica continued with her ministrations. It was hard work, and after ten minutes she had to stop and take a deep breath. She was perspiring almost as much as Lyle, her thin top sticking uncomfortably to her skin, her scalp prickling with heat.

He made a sound deep in his throat, the moment her hands left his skin, that her senses recognised as a form of protest, and automatically she bent towards him again, this time working on his shoulders and the mass of compacted muscles just below them, her fingers cautious at first and then firmer as she felt the slight slackening in tension that registered his body's acceptance of her touch.

It was hot, hard work; much harder work than massaging her mother, whose muscles had not possessed the unyielding hardness of Lyle's. The overpoweringly muggy heat of the afternoon didn't help and the perspiration that had prickled her scalp now ran damply over her skin to gather in a single bead that dropped down onto to Lyle's shoulder as she bent over him.

Not wanting to break the soothing rhythm of her fingers to wipe it away, in an uncalculated, automatic movement Jessica bent her head delicately absorbing the moisture with her tongue.

Her reaction was governed only by an instinctive need not to break the relaxed tenor of his breathing, nor to disturb what she knew would be over-sensitive nerve endings, but the moment her tongue touched the hot flesh of his shoulder she knew how misinterpreted her actions could be. She had forgotten for a moment that he was an adult male, and one moreover who had been coldly clinical about his lack of desire for her, his vulnerability and pain arousing inside her much the same sort of compassion and concern she felt for Stuart and James, but these weren't things she could easily explain to him, she realised sickly as she felt his body tense beneath her fingers, his head lifting off the pillow and turning so that his eyes were looking directly into her own, dark with…with what? Anger? Disbelief? Distaste?

She was just about to apologise and try to explain when he said in a voice that was curiously light and totally devoid of all emotion, 'I think you'd better go.'

His eyes were already closing, blotting out the sight of her, Jessica thought numbly, horribly aware of the tide of scarlet heat surging up through her body. Did he think that she had been trying to make him aware of her? To arouse him? As her fingers left his skin she shuddered in a mixture of despair and anger. Surely he knew her well enough by now to know that she simply wasn't that sort of woman? That to invade his privacy when he was ill and defenceless, especially for so stupid and senseless a reason, simply was not in her?

But what other interpretation could he put on her actions? Now what she had done, far from being an automatic instinctive reaction, seemed to be the most crassly foolish thing she had ever done in her life. As she straightened up and moved away from his body, fully aware, despite the fact that his eyes were closed, that he was far from being asleep it came to her on a wave of anguish that by her stupidity she had destroyed the rapport that had been building up between them over the last few weeks.

She was outside his room, closing the door quietly behind her before it occurred to her to ask herself why she should feel such acute pain at the thought of losing what at best was no more than a cool acceptance of her.

It was a question she did not wish to answer, instead spending what was left of the evening constructing various explanations of the truth which she could offer him once he was fully recovered, but knowing that she would be far better advised simply to let the matter drop. It was far more sensible; far, far safer simply to pretend indifference to his opinion and reaction, and to wait instead for him to bring the matter up if he chose.

'JESSICA?'

She recognised Justine's voice immediately she answered the phone.

'How's everything going?' her sister-in-law enquired when they had exchanged 'hellos'.

'Better than I'd hoped, at least as far as the boys are concerned.'

'But that brother of mine's giving you problems, is that it?' Justine sympathised. 'He always was a stubborn so-and-so, and could never admit to being in the wrong. I remember when he married Heather. I told him then it would never work out. She was so obviously not the sort of girl to be put on a pedestal. She wanted a career, not the life of a housewife with babies, but Lyle would never admit that I was right—at least not until after the divorce. He tried everything to make that marriage work, but Heather just wasn't interested. I suspect that's what makes him a bit ''anti'' where our sex is concerned, but I had hoped by now that he would have come to realise the benefits of being married.'

'Oh, I think he does accept that there are benefits,' Jessica responded guardedly. 'In fact I suspect it's more the loaded revolver that was held to his head that he resents.' That and the fact that it was her he had had to marry, Jessica added mentally, but that was something she was not prepared to admit to Lyle's sister, no matter how well they got on.

'Oh dear, still sulking, is he? I'd hoped he'd be over that by now. Oliver, my husband, is due home tomorrow, it's his birthday on Saturday and I'm trying to arrange a party for him. I was hoping that all of you could come over, and your sister and her husband too, if they can. With the weather being so good, I've been thinking in terms of a barbecue in the garden, kicking off about lunchtime and going on for as long as we feel like it.'

'Well, I'd certainly like to come,' Jessica told her, 'and so I'm sure will the boys. I'm not so sure about Andrea and David. David normally plays golf at the weekend, and of course Lyle could well be on call, but I'll check with him.'

A little to her surprise, Andrea when the invitation was passed on to her rang back within half an hour to announce that both she and David would be there.

'After all we haven't met any of Lyle's family yet,' she pointed out to Jessica, making the latter smile a little to herself.

'Well, since we've been married for two months now, it's a little late to start checking into his background,' she teased her sister.

Lyle too confirmed that he would be free that afternoon. The slight coolness that had sprung up between them since he had his migraine attack made Jessica feel nervously hesitant about approaching him; the way his mouth tightened slightly in derision whenever she had to ask him anything betrayed his own awareness of her edginess. He had never once referred to what had happened that evening but it lay between them, a sword, sharp and dangerous to whoever should try to pick it up, and yet Jessica would have liked to talk about it, if only to clear the air.

She became suffused with heat and guilt every time she considered the interpretation he must have put on her actions and was now doubly careful about keeping her distance from him. Only this morning their fingers had touched accidentally as she was handing him his coffee and she had retreated from the contact as though burned, hating the derisory smile that curled his mouth as he watched her.

It said a great deal for the progress she had made with Stuart and James that both of them had quite cheerfully agreed to attend the barbecue lunch, Stuart albeit less readily than James. It cheered her to see how much both of them had grown in self-confidence and security, especially Stuart, who had been so prickly and withdrawn the first time she had seen him.

'Will you always be with us?' he had asked her only that morning and she had replied as honestly as she could.

'I hope so, Stuart. I want to be.'

How could she explain to him that she doubted that his father wanted her as a permanent feature in his life? It had depressed her to see the small shadow of pain and wariness momentarily darkening his eyes.

He seemed to have recovered quite quickly though, and had been cheerful enough when she took them both swimming later.

CHAPTER SIX

THE HEAT STILL HUNG in the summer air like a miasma on Saturday morning when Jessica got up. The kitchen felt oppressively hot and she half wished she had not offered to contribute a raspberry soufflé to the barbecue lunch.

Lyle had some calls to make and disappeared immediately after breakfast. As always, Jessica experienced an easing of her disturbing inner tension when he had gone, and after shooing both boys out into the garden she started making her soufflé. She was just about to pour the mixture into its collared soufflé-dish to set when Stuart came in.

'It's too hot to play,' he complained, scowling as he added, 'do we really have to go to Aunt Justine's? I'd rather stay here.'

Putting down her bowl, Jessica studied his down-bent head. She was aware of the problems that had existed between Justine's son and his cousins, and could well understand Stuart's reluctance to return to the scene of the crime so to speak, and even sympathised with it to some extent, but this was one of those occasions when for his own good she knew she would have to be firm.

'If you stay it would be rather rude, especially as your uncle will be there. He hasn't seen you for a long time, has he? I know it's hot,' she continued, smiling a little as she added persuasively, 'how would you like it if we went in my car? We could put the hood down and that will help you to cool off.'

She could see that he was tempted, and was glad that she hadn't fallen into the trap of insisting that he should accompany them.

'What's that you're making?' he asked her, changing the subject.

'Raspberry soufflé. Want a taste?'

When he nodded his head, she found a clean tea-spoon and scooped up some of the mixture, handing the spoon to him. The look of sheer pleasure on his face as he licked it clean made her laugh, and she was still smiling when Lyle walked in through the back door.

'God, it's hot out there. We're in for a storm soon, I suspect. What time are we due at Justine's?' he asked, frowning slightly as he glanced at his watch.

'Twelve,' Jessica told him, deftly pouring the soufflé into the dish and carrying it across to the refrigerator. By the time they were ready to leave it would be set, and just to be on the safe side she would put it into a coolbag to transport it.

'Dad, just have a taste of this,' Stuart exhorted his father. 'It's great.'

'Raspberry soufflé,' Jessica explained in response to the enquiring look Lyle gave her over his son's head. 'Justine asked me to make it.'

'Let Dad taste it,' Stuart urged her.

Feeling unaccountably nervous, Jessica got a clean teaspoon and scraped it along the side of the empty bowl. Lyle had come to stand beside her, and as always she felt her muscles clench, her nerve endings vibrating in acute awareness of his proximity.

She had intended merely to hand Lyle the spoon, but somehow as she tried to pass it to him, his fingers became entangled with hers, closing firmly over them. Even so, the shock of being touched by him made her hand shake so much that half the contents of the heaped spoon ended up on her fingers. Unable to pull away, she tried not to watch the slow curl of Lyle's tongue as he cleaned the spoon, her stomach abruptly compressing with shock as he removed the spoon and then lifted her sticky fingers to his mouth, first licking away the spilled soufflé and then slowly sucking her fingers clean.

A sensation unlike anything she had ever experienced in her life before sheeted through her, her body paralysed as she simply stood there in amazed shock, unable to move away. She felt as though her entire body had turned to liquid, as though she was about to dissolve completely and escape the material cage of her flesh.

It seemed unbelievable that such a simple and automatic reaction on his part should have such a devastating effect on her senses. The minute his tongue had touched her skin her stomach had dropped like a high-speed lift, while her pulse rate had accelerated way, way past its normal level.

Now as he released her hand it was impossible for her to look away from him, even though she desperately wanted to conceal from him what she had experienced.

Stuart might just as well not have been there for all the attention Lyle paid him as he said softly to her, 'Now we're equal.'

Equal? What was he talking about? Her brain felt sluggish and heavy as though somehow it had been drugged. Stuart had to speak to her twice before she realised he had said anything, and even then it was several seconds before she could pull herself together sufficiently to agree that it was time that he and James went upstairs to shower and change.

'Don't forget you promised we could go in your car,' he reminded her as he shot out into the garden.

Lyle was watching her. She could tell, even with her back to him, simply by the way the skin at the base of her skull prickled.

'It isn't nice being aroused when you can't do a damn thing about it, is it, Jessica?'

She spun round staring at him, shock coursing through her veins. 'Now you know how I felt the other day,' he continued harshly. 'What the hell did you think you were doing? Surely you can't have forgotten the rules already?'

His voice was so bitterly derisory that it took her some time to realise what he meant, and when she did her face flamed hotly. He didn't think that she had deliberately... But he did, she realised swiftly, and what's more he was so furiously angry about it that he had deliberately set out to punish her.

Anger fought with guilt and shock as she tried to blot out the fierce surge of desire that had kicked through her body when he touched her, wanting to deny to herself how she had felt but totally unable to do so.

The silence in the kitchen seemed to stretch interminably as she searched feverishly for the right response. One that would make it plain to him that she never had, nor ever would have any desire to arouse him, but somehow she could not find the words, and had to content herself with a tightly defensive, 'You're quite wrong, but I don't suppose it matters what I say, you won't believe me. Anyway,' she added almost childishly, 'you told me before you married that you weren't capable of being aroused.'

'A bad mistake,' he agreed cuttingly. 'I'd forgotten your sex's unfortunate predilection for anything even remotely resembling a challenge. You must either like making things difficult for yourself or be so sure of your skills that you felt the need to add a handicap if you ever seriously believed it might be possible to arouse a man in the state I was in.'

His insinuations literally took her breath away, or rather the hard knot of anger that was gathering inside her chest was so huge that it all but choked her, making speech totally impossible. Inwardly she was fuming; and for the first time in her life Jessica realised why it was that some women felt the need to resort to acts of childish violence when confronted with an argument with a man. Right now there was nothing she would enjoy more than hurling the baking bowl at the arrogant dark head, but fortunately she managed to retain just enough sanity and self-control to withstand the impulse.

Turning her back on him, she took off her protective apron and said curtly, 'I'm going to wash up and then I'm going upstairs to get ready. If you prefer to drive to Justine's on your own, I quite understand.'

She could tell from the sound of his voice that his mouth had hardened, even without turning to look, and she shivered to realise how intimately she must have observed him on a thousand unrealised occasions to know with such certainty what physical expression any certain nuance in his voice represented.

Two hours later they were all ready. Both boys

were dressed in clean T-shirts and jeans worn over their bathing trunks, since Lyle had explained that his sister's garden possessed a small although unheated swimming pool. Lyle himself was wearing close-fitting stone-washed jeans in an indeterminate colour somewhere between olive and stone with a matching shirt, the sleeves rolled up and the buttons unfastened halfway down his chest.

Jessica was the last to appear downstairs, to be greeted by a malely impatient 'Hooray' from James.

She now knew exactly why mothers were always the last to be ready, having had her own preparations constantly interrupted by cries of 'Where are my new jeans/T-shirt/favourite socks?'

Now she was ready however, and her aqua cotton jeans and matching T-shirt drew a totally unexpected and slightly embarrassed compliment from Stuart, which she accepted gravely, hiding a tiny smile at James's robust and brotherly, 'It's soppy telling girls that they look nice.'

She turned automatically to look at Lyle, her smile fading as she saw that he was frowning. For a moment she had almost forgotten their passage of arms in the kitchen. Deriding herself for ever having expected him to share in her covert amusement, as though they were in fact two adults intimately united in amused pride of their offspring, she hurried over to the refrigerator extracting the soufflé and deftly placing it in the coolbag.

'Why's it got that paper round it?' James asked curiously, watching her, listening as she explained the purpose of the grease-proof collar.

Lyle was the last to leave the house, and Jessica fully expected him to walk over to his own car once he had locked the door.

She unlocked her car and waited while James and Stuart put their towels in the boot, and was just about to get in when she realised that Lyle had joined them.

She hesitated, torn between offering to let him drive and the wilful urge not to. Why should she go out of her way to placate him? To do what he as a man no doubt expected her to do? It was her car, she reminded herself sturdily, inwardly acknowledging as she swung her door open that had they not had that quarrel earlier, she would probably never have even thought twice about offering to let him drive.

Pushing down the back of her seat she helped the boys clamber into the back, and then got in closing the door and starting the engine.

Lyle, who had been standing by the boot, got into the passenger seat without any comment. It was impossible to tell from where he had been standing whether he had expected to drive or not, but Jessica suspected that he must have done. In her experience very few men could endure being driven by a woman, especially when that woman was the man's wife. Even so, he made no comment as she backed out of the drive and turned the car in the right direction.

As she had predicted, having the hood down produced a deliciously cooling breeze, which since she had already taken the precaution of restraining her hair did not cause her any inconvenience.

They had the narrow country roads almost entirely to themselves, the boys keeping up a steady flow of chatter for the first few miles, although Lyle was completely silent. When she had the opportunity to take her eyes off the road and dart a brief glance at him, Jessica was chagrined to discover that he appeared to be fast asleep, his head turned away from her, his body moving easily with the car, his long legs stretched out it in front of him.

'Dad's gone to sleep,' James commented, confirming her own suspicions.

So much for her determination not to let him drive! Almost she was grinding her teeth, resenting the way he seemed to have got the better of her. The childishness of her thoughts almost made her smile. What a ridiculous way to behave! She was supposed to be an adult; mature; her research and qualifications such that she of all people ought to have been able to anticipate and avoid the hazards of emotionally explosive situations, instead of which she appeared to be acting like a text-book case designed to reveal what the male sex commonly held to be the weaknesses of the feminine psyche. Frowning slightly, Jessica remembered how smugly superior she had felt in the past whenever Andrea had indignantly related to her how easily David could upset and irritate her. But Andrea was vulnerable because she loved David, and she, Jessica, had long ago seen how potentially dangerous and threatening loving a man could be to a woman who wished to retain her independence and self-respect. Love involved giving, bending, becoming pliant and responsive to another's needs and desires. And wasn't it because of that, and the terrible emotional devastation that could be wrought when one person ceased to love another, that she had turned away from the modern romantic ideal of love and turned instead towards the past and its more prosaic and firmer-founded alliances based on less ephemeral bonds?

She shivered, goosebumps puckering her skin even though she was not really cold.

Lyle woke up just as they were turning into Justine's drive, stretching slowly and then sitting up. Had he really been asleep, or had he guessed why she had insisted on driving and pretended to be asleep accordingly?

Unless she asked him she was never likely to know, she reflected wryly as she stopped the car and got out.

She was just helping the boys out of the back

when Justine appeared, a burly, deeply tanned, fair-haired man at her side.

Watching them together as Oliver greeted Lyle and then hugged both boys, Jessica was struck by the very evident affection that existed between them, something she had not expected from Justine's offhand manner of mentioning her husband whenever he came into the conversation.

'And this is Jessica?'

'Ah ha, saving the best for last?' Oliver grinned at her and then looked at Lyle asking, 'Will I be safe if I kiss her?'

'From me, yes,' Lyle drawled in response, smiling mockingly at his sister as he added teasingly, 'from Justine, I'm not so sure.'

For the first time since she and Lyle had married Jessica felt excluded; alien; overwhelmed by a deep sense of melancholy she was at a loss to understand.

She had got what she wanted from their marriage, and more; the boys' affection for her was an added bonus. So why was she feeling so bereft?

'Come on into the garden.' Justine looked beyond her husband and brother and smiled at Jessica. 'That looks like the soufflé. I'll take it inside, shall I?'

While Oliver led Lyle and the boys round the side of the house to the back garden Jessica followed Justine inside.

Her kitchen overlooked the brick-paved area where they were having the barbecue and Justine grimaced faintly as she watched her son belly-flop into the pool and send a cascade of water up on to the terrace.

'Little horror! It's just as well Oliver's home. He was beginning to get out of hand. Too much petti-coat-government, Oliver says.' She grinned again and added cheerfully, 'Chauvinist.' There wasn't the slightest trace of resentment in her voice and Jessica was frankly puzzled. The very first time she had met Justine she had been struck by her forceful, direct manner, and yet here she was apparently quite con-tent—no, not merely content, but almost pleased—to hand over the reins of control to Oliver. And from the little she had seen of the latter, Jessica could not see him being a man who would wish or allow his wife to dominate him.

Almost as though she had been reading her mind Justine said resignedly, 'I know what you're think-ing, Oliver and I are far too alike to be happily mar-ried, and perhaps we wouldn't be if he didn't spend so much time away working. As it is, when he does come back I'm quite happy to relax into the role of little woman and let him take charge. And Oliver, of course, is so used to being in command and tell-ing others what to do that he wouldn't take very kindly to a subservient role, I'm afraid. Even so one thing I will say for him is that he's always willing to sit down and discuss any points of dispute. Unlike Lyle, he doesn't have a temper.' She pulled a face and admitted wryly, 'Sometimes I wish he did have, I have to admit it gives me great pleasure to pull the tiger's tail sometimes, especially where Lyle's concerned. He gives such a magnificent lashing reaction, very male and affronted.' Her eyes danced and Jessica couldn't help grinning in response.

'Oh ho, I think I hear a car,' Justine announced. 'Maybe it's your sister. I won't be a sec.'

It was Andrea, looking glowingly pregnant, and David, scowling slightly as he followed her and William into the kitchen.

'I think I'm about finished in here. Let's go out into the garden and get a drink,' Justine suggested, shepherding them all towards the door.

She was magnificently organised, Jessica acknowledged, observing the crisp salads set out on the long trestle table.

'Everyone's here now,' Justine announced. 'I think you'd better start barbecuing, Oliver, before the kids get too tired and hungry.' She stopped to smile at William and then took him over to introduce him to her own son, leaving Oliver to make sure that everyone had drinks.

As far as everyone else was concerned, lunch seemed to be an unmarred success. Even Andrea looked unusually relaxed; only she seemed unable to settle, Jessica thought morosely, watching as all four boys stripped off jeans and T-shirts and headed for the pool.

'God, where do they get their energy?' Oliver commented watching them.

'Do you really want to know?' Justine riposted. 'At the last count Peter had consumed at least four beefburgers, plus ice cream, plus raspberry soufflé.'

'Don't tell me any more,' Oliver begged, eyeing his son's wiry body as he added plaintively, 'if he eats as much as that, how come he's so thin?' He eyed his own sturdy waistline wryly and added, 'I only have to look at ice cream...'

'Peter is thin because he works it off. Exercise is the thing,' Justine told him reprovingly.

Only half listening to their bantering, Jessica watched the pool. Lyle was with the boys and they were perfectly safe, but in any case it was not they that drew her eye but Lyle himself. White swimming-shorts moulded his body, his skin sleek and tautly muscled as he hauled himself up out of the pool.

Her breath seemed to catch in her throat, her whole body reverberating with a kind of pain that ripped apart the flimsy delusion she had been hiding behind.

From a distance she heard Andrea speaking to her and turned her head towards her sister in mute enquiry.

'I was just apologising for being such a fool about David,' she laughed softly and then added, 'even if I hadn't already realised how silly I'd been, just see-

ing you look at Lyle the way you were doing then
would have told me. I never thought I'd see the day
when you were so deeply in love that you couldn't
tear your eyes away from a man, Jess.'

Somewhere deep inside her the pain grew and
spread, crying out a silent denial, her body shuddering with reaction and shock.

'Jess?' Concern quickened Andrea's voice, her
hand reaching out to touch her. 'Are you all right?'

'It's the heat, it made me feel dizzy, that's all.'

Instantly Andrea gave her a speculative look.
'You're not...'

Sensing what was coming, Jessica quickly shook
her head. Andrea thought she was pregnant! My
God, if only her sister knew the irony of what she
was suggesting. It was as impossible for her to be
pregnant as it was for her to love Lyle. Slowly her
mind faltered to a standstill, her stomach churning
restlessly. She got up, filled with a sudden need to
escape from the others; to be alone somewhere quiet
where she could sort out her confused thoughts.

While Andrea's attention was distracted by William she got up and walked quickly away, heading
for the lower end of the garden.

A trellis smothered in old-fashioned perfumed
roses separated the lawns from a small orchard area.
As she leaned against the trunk of one of the trees
the sounds of muted laughter and splashing from the
pool seemed to belong to another world. She was,

she recognised shakily, suffering from acute shock, her skin clammy to her own touch, her body icy cold inside despite the smotheringly oppressive heat of the afternoon. All at once her nerve-endings felt raw and exposed, her skin too thin and sensitive to bear the atmospheric pressure crushing down on it. She felt hot and cold at the same time, crampingly sick and totally unable to come to terms with the truth that hammered remorselessly inside her head, demanding acknowledgement.

She was no longer an island, complete within herself, able to exist and function wholly without the necessity of having another person with whom to share her life. Without her knowing how it had happened Lyle had pierced the defensive bubble inside which she had thought herself so safely encapsulated. To describe the onset of anguish and anger that possessed her when she tried to contemplate her life without him as 'love' came nowhere near encompassing the intensity of her feelings.

Fool, fool, she cursed herself inwardly, knowing now that the signs had been there for her to read almost from the first time she set eyes on him, but she had blindly, even wilfully, deliberately ignored them.

That immediate, and yes, half-intoxicating antipathy she had experienced and ignored; that alone should have warned her. Amused indifference was her normal reaction to angry males, and she had known enough of them. Men often became angry when they discovered how impervious she was to them.

She had not simply married him because of Andrea, she was forced to recognise that now and although she had not consciously formed her decision on the strength of their first meeting, subconsciously...

She stiffened as she heard footsteps on the brick path. Had Lyle noticed her absence and come after her? The sharpness of her disappointment when she realised that the intruder was David increased her annoyance with herself. It was insupportable that a woman with her training and knowledge should have been stupid enough to do the one thing she herself, in her books, preached against so earnestly. It was her own thoughts rather than David's presence that made her twist uncomfortably against the tree. Jessica had always prided herself on her honesty and her very real belief in what she wrote, and now she was being forced to confront the fact that she herself had fallen helplessly into the trap Nature wove so treacherously for the unwary. She did not even have the excuse of having been encouraged to love Lyle. After all, he had made no bones at all about his feelings towards her—or rather his lack of them.

'Well, well, all alone without your new husband. What interpretation are we to put on that, I wonder?'

As always, David's slightly unctuous manner irritated her. Today of all days she felt ill-inclined to humour him and instead snapped crossly, 'None at all, David. I simply wanted some peace and quiet,' she told him pointedly.

He laughed, or sniggered rather, and mentally Jessica contrasted the grating effect of that sound on her eardrums when compared with the richness and warmth of Lyle's laughter. Not that she had heard it very often, of course, and when she had it had been generated by one or other of his sons.

Stop being so maudlin, she berated herself, moving away from the tree-trunk intent on rejoining the others. She had no wish to stay here alone with David of all people.

'Not so fast.' His arm across the arched opening through the rose trellis prevented her from going through, but before she had had time to form the scathing rebuke rising to her lips, he continued silkily, 'Andrea will have it that you're desperately in love with your rather dour husband, but you and I know better, don't we, Jess? You aren't capable of love, it's against all those high-minded principles of yours. You married him to stop Andrea from finding out about us.'

He was so close to the truth and yet so far away from it, that Jessica was tempted to laugh. If he had confronted her with those words only a matter of days ago she would have agreed, albeit with some modifications; but now she knew just how wrong he was, and ironically how very much she wished that he might have been right.

Even so, it gave her a degree of rather wry pleasure to be able to say to him quite honestly, 'You're wrong, David, I do love him.'

She held his eyes and had the satisfaction of seeing his glance drop away first, but not before she had seen the sudden flare of rage spring to life in them.

All at once she was acutely conscious of how secluded they were, and as though somehow in loving Lyle she had become acutely vulnerable in a way she had not experienced before, suddenly she was uneasily aware that she might have been wiser not to push David quite so hard.

'You bitch! You enjoyed telling me that, didn't you?'

Breathing hard, he grabbed her with painful fingers that dug into her arms and refused to release her no matter how hard she tried to push him off. The pressure of his mouth against her own nauseated and affronted her. She kicked out wildly at his shin, but it was not her own frantic attempts to evade him that brought her freedom, but Lyle's totally unexpected presence, his face blackly grim as he said curtly to David, 'I think you'd better go back to your wife.'

To Jessica's relief, her brother-in-law made no attempt to argue, simply going back the way he had come.

Her heart was pumping frantically, her whole body shaking. She was just about to thank Lyle for coming to her rescue when he said grittily, 'Couldn't you even have the decency to wait for a more propitious moment? I'm no fool, Jessica,' he told her when she would have interrupted. 'Did you honestly think I believed for one moment that tale you spun me about him? You may not be lovers right now, but it's plain to me that you have been. But if you think you will be again, let me tell you right here and now that it won't be while you're married to me. For God's sake,' he demanded rawly, 'what the hell did you think you were playing at? Anyone could have come down here and seen you, your sister for one, the boys for another. Did you stop to think what that might have done to them? No. You didn't think about a damn thing apart from satisfying your own lust, did you? And don't tell me there was more to it than that, Jessica. You've already told me that you don't believe in love, so what else could it possibly be?'

She was still shaking, but not with shock now but anger.

'Nothing to say?' His mouth twisted as he watched her, his eyes condemning her.

'Plenty,' she told him shakily, at last. 'But since you already seem to have condemned me without waiting to hear it, there doesn't seem to be any point.'

Without waiting to see what his response was, she pushed past him and fled back to the others.

They were all sitting round the pool, a very chastened David standing by Andrea's chair.

'Ah, there you are,' her sister smiled at her. 'Lyle was getting quite concerned about you.' She turned her head to smile at David. 'It quite takes me back, darling. Remember when we were first married?'

Only someone who was completely blind could surely think that Lyle had been driven to seek her because he wanted her company, Jessica thought, looking at her husband's grim face.

'I think we'd better make tracks, Jus,' she heard him saying to his sister. 'The weather doesn't look too promising, and I don't want to get caught in a storm on the way back.'

The sky did look ominous, but Jessica was not deceived. She knew why she was being hurried away like a recalcitrant child, and so, she suspected, did Justine, although the latter admittedly said nothing to her as she accompanied them all out to the car, Oliver coming with her, and standing with his arm draped round her shoulders as they made their farewells.

This time Lyle drove, getting into the driver's seat before she could challenge him for possession of it.

He was a good driver, she acknowledged, all his

attention apparently concentrated on his driving, but before they were home, they could hear the first ominous growls of thunder in the distance.

It continued to thunder all evening, low, spasmodic rumbles, the odd flash of lightning illuminating the unnaturally dark sky.

The boys were tired after their games in the pool and settled down quite happily after supper to play chess. Jessica had expected Lyle to take himself off to do some work, but to her consternation he remained in the sitting-room with them.

At nine o'clock she had to suppress a cowardly desire to give in to the boys' entreaties to be allowed to stay up for a while. Even so, she managed to drag out the routine of getting them into bed until just after ten. As she went back downstairs, having wished them both good night, she found herself hoping that the sitting-room would be empty.

To her relief it was. Lyle must have gone into his surgery to do some work. With him gone she felt able to breathe properly for the first time that evening.

Shivering a little, she went to the window and watched the approaching storm, gathering momentum now, the thunder drawing ever closer. Storms had never frightened her, on the contrary she found them strangely invigorating, but tonight she was not in the right frame of mind, already far too tense and wound up by the events of the afternoon. She felt as edgy as an animal sensing danger, she thought wryly, acknowledging that her most sensible course would be to remove herself from the possibility of encountering Lyle by going to bed.

Switching off the light she made her way upstairs, pushing open the door of her bedroom and then coming to an abrupt halt.

Lyle was standing by the window, apparently watching the storm as she had been doing earlier. Suddenly her throat was so constricted she could barely breathe, her 'what are you doing in here?' coming out as an agonised croak.

'Waiting for you.' He had swung round as she walked in, but with his face in the shadows and his voice devoid of all emotion it was impossible to guess at his mood.

CHAPTER SEVEN

'WAITING FOR *ME*?' Unlike his her voice vibrated with her feelings. 'Why? To apologise for your totally unfounded accusations this afternoon?'

Mild hysteria cramped her stomach as he turned and she saw his face. His voice had deceived her—totally—she could see now that he was blazingly, furiously angry.

'Apologise? For what? Preventing you from sating your lust for physical satisfaction?'

It was the ugly, jeering sound of his voice that did it, that and the derogatory look in his eyes. She flew at him like a wildcat, raising her hand to strike his face and then when the grip of his fingers manacling her wrist prevented her, using her nails instead.

She heard the indrawn hiss of his breath and felt him recoil with a savage sense of pleasure. The thunder outside seemed to be echoed by the tumultuous pounding of her blood as it beat through her body. She was in the grip of a feeling as primitive and elemental as the storm itself, too intent on her own fierce need to draw blood to even think of the consequences until she found herself flat on her back on her bed, with Lyle bending over her, his face contorted in a mask of rage.

It was his need to punish her for daring to attack her that was responsible for the indignity of her present position; sprawled out on her bed, with the heavy weight of Lyle's body keeping her there, his breathing harsh and uneven, whether from rage or exertion she wasn't quite sure. She squirmed beneath him, her own anger burning as high as his, and then stilled in mute shock as she felt his body's reaction to her.

For a moment as their glances tangled in mutual recognition it seemed to Jessica that he too was shocked and then the shock was gone and his hands were on her shoulders, pinning her against the bed, his mouth fierce and bitter as it took hers.

Close at hand now the thunder crashed and rolled, its urgency mirrored in the febrile excitement heating her blood. She could tell that Lyle felt it too. His mouth moved on hers in relentless, feverish need that her mind told her had nothing to do with any gentle emotion, but which her body, fiercely exultant, would not let her heed.

She felt Lyle's hands slide down her rib cage, gripping her almost bruisingly as he tugged her T-shirt free of her jeans, and part of her brain fought free of desire long enough for her to register how much she wanted the touch of his hands against her skin.

Her body arched willingly, helping him to remove her thin top and bra.

Now it was almost dark outside, the lightning that suddenly split the sky almost overhead illuminating her naked breasts, turning her skin a pagan gold.

She heard the tormented, aroused sound of Lyle's indrawn breath, her body quivering on the verge of intense pleasure as he cupped her breasts, holding them as reverently as though they were indeed made of that most precious of metals.

Strangely, even while he touched her one part of her knew that like her, tonight he was a different person transformed by his earlier anger. Tomorrow... But she would not think of that now. She would not even think beyond the exquisite pleasure of the look in Lyle's eyes as he stared down at her.

Oddly, she felt no embarrassment or awkwardness, rather a heightened sense of acceptance; of knowing from the moment she had first seen him that this would happen. And now that it had, with the knowledge of her love for him still fresh in her mind she felt able to abandon herself completely to the fiercely drugging desire heating her veins without either guilt or regret.

'Beautiful...you're so beautiful.'

Lyle's voice was slow and slurred, the tension in his body like that of a man in a trance, and then when, acting on an impulse totally new to her, Jessica arched her spine slightly, pressing her breasts tormentingly into the warmth of his palms, she saw that tension break, his body shivering with reaction as he bent his head and drew the hard peak of one breast into the heat of his mouth.

Both the caress and the sensations it aroused were new to her, the shock-wave of pleasure convulsing her, making her moan huskily and cling to his shoulders while wave after wave of delight rippled through her. Her one previous lover had not been interested in any form of love-play, and although she had read and heard about it, nothing had prepared her for the intensity of it.

Now she was shivering too, digging her nails into the smooth muscles of Lyle's back as she fought to hold on to reality and to ignore the deep aching pressure building up low in her body, activated by the feverishly urgent tug of Lyle's mouth on her breast. Her skin was so sensitised and aroused that she could feel the faint abrasion of his jaw, and when at last he released her aching nipple she clung to him, not wanting the pleasure to cease, frightened that somehow the spell might have been broken and that Lyle had realised what he was doing and with whom—because she was convinced that he had been so caught off guard by his own physical desire that he had not yet realised who she was—at least not consciously. To her relief instead of drawing away he turned his attention to her other breast, muttering thickly into her skin.

'Did you like that? Did it make you feel good? You taste of honey, did you know that?'

All the time his mouth was moving closer to the pink aureole of her nipple, pressing soft kisses into the smooth skin of her breast as his hand cupped its twin.

Wholly unable to articulate any response, Jessica did all she could to communicate to him the frantic urgency building up inside her, arching her spine, making small sounds of need deep in her throat that ended in a sob of release as his tongue ceased teasing her aching flesh and his mouth closed satisfyingly around it.

This time the pleasure was even greater, piercing her almost painfully so that she sobbed his name beneath her breath and moved instinctively beneath him, wanting to get as close as she could to the hard throb of his body.

When he eased himself away from her slightly, she cried out in denial, reaching down between their bodies to curl her fingers around his wrist, her tension slackening only when she discovered that he was easing down the zip of his jeans.

His mouth still caressed her breast, and realising he was not after all going to leave her, she started to relax, releasing her grip, but it seemed he had mistaken her intentions and as she pulled away his fingers entwined with hers and then placed her hand against the taut flesh of his belly.

Beneath her fingertips she could feel the faint abrasion of body hair. She could also feel the tension within him. He moved, placing his lips against her ear, his jeans sliding free of his body as he muttered rawly, 'Touch me...'

He shuddered as her hand moved across his body in immediate response. The fingers of one of his hands were curled into her shoulder, while the other dealt with her own zip.

The moment she felt the heat of his hand just above the line where her narrow briefs finished, she knew exactly what had made him utter that raw, tormented demand, and it was all the more shocking when suddenly he pushed her hand away and sat up with his back to her, his skin gleaming satin-gold in the half-light.

Unbelievably the thunder seemed to have stopped, but she had been so wrapped up in her desire for him that she had not even been aware of it. But now it was over. Lyle, it seemed, had realised what he was doing. She started to sit up herself, and then checked, slow quivers of nervous excitement building up inside her as she realised that Lyle wasn't leaving her; he was simply removing the rest of his clothes.

As he came back to her the thin light fell directly across his body, aroused and undeniably male. She wanted to reach out and touch him, Jessica realised, recognising within herself a primitive and very strong urge to worship and embrace the maleness of him, not so much in desire as in a wholly feminine need to pay homage to him as a male source of life.

It was a revelationary moment, illuminating for her an aspect of her own nature she had never guessed existed. To kneel before him and caress the male contours of his body might seem to others to be an act of humility and recognition of his male superiority, but Jessica knew that it wasn't that. It was more a need to acknowledge the power and perfection of him, fashioned so specifically to complement and complete her own femininity.

Her hands were on his thighs before she was even aware of moving. Beneath her fingertips his muscles felt like corded steel, his body so immobile it was almost as though he were afraid to move.

She glanced up and saw in his face acute torment and acute desire and suddenly realised just what she was doing to him. She started to withdraw, her breath rattling in her lungs as his hands dug into her shoulders, her sense of reality totally swept away as he groaned a tortured denial. He wanted her to touch him.

Slowly, delicately she did so until their mutual calm was shattered by desire. Jessica could feel it pulsing through his body, thudding openly through his veins and held tightly under control as he thrust her hands away from him, gripping her fingers so tightly that she felt they might break as he fought for control.

'No...' The sound was almost strangled in his throat, the muscles clenched and ridging. 'Not like this...not yet... I want you... I want you, Jessica.'

He had said her name. He knew who she was. His recognition of her half-shocked her into immobility, awareness only flooding back as she felt him removing her jeans.

Her body was not something she had ever given much thought to in the past, but now suddenly she was anxious about it, and she stiffened in tension as he removed her briefs and looked down at her. For a second the silence was something she could almost feel pressing down on her, and then she heard Lyle sigh and the tension was broken.

'You're so beautiful.'

His hands stroked over her skin, gentle and yet scorching her where they touched, making her ache with the torment of all that they promised and yet still withheld. She wanted him. She wanted him now, and in the most primitive and intense way it was possible for a woman to want a man.

'Jessica.' He said her name against her ear, lying down and taking her into his arms, his voice muffled and strained. 'I can't make love to you the way I wanted to...I can't wait that long. I want you, now.'

Jessica wasn't sure which of them had said it, she

only knew that as he moved and fitted her beneath his body there was nothing she wanted more than to feel him deep inside her.

And yet despite the intensity with which she had wanted him there was still a momentary sensation of discomfort, of tightness, quickly dispelled as her body adapted itself to him. Of course it had been a long time, and even then nothing, nothing like this. And then her thoughts turned hazy and finally had to be abandoned as her body picked up the rhythm his was imposing on it, matched it and gloried in it, her legs wrapped tightly round him as she sought to draw him deeper and deeper within her.

The pulsing, demanding pressure that had been building up inside her from the moment he touched her gathered strength and grew, her body slick with sweat as she arched breathlessly against him and felt the bubble of pleasure explode and expand in a series of pulsing ripples that Lyle's climax caught at their height and intensified to such a pitch that for a moment she almost felt as though she had actually fainted.

Now with the last residue of pleasure gently washing through her body she was reluctantly coming down to earth. Now the caution she would not acknowledge earlier came crashing down over her, and as Lyle moved away from her and the harsh sound of his breathing started to ease slightly she wondered in appalled comprehension just what interpretation he would put on her behaviour. At all costs he must not guess that she loved him! If he did he was all too likely to send her away, and that was something she could not endure. She had broken the most important of the rules governing their marriage, and now she must try to repair the damage before Lyle started putting two and two together and came up with four.

It cost her everything she had to appear detached and say calmly, 'I thought you couldn't do that.'

She felt Lyle's momentary tension without having to look at him. The mattress moved slightly as he levered himself up on one elbow, and knowing that he was watching her Jessica turned her head. In the dim light it was impossible for her to read his expression, but his voice was even calmer than hers as he retorted drily, 'It seems that anger is a very effective aphrodisiac.'

So now she knew. He had not made love to her out of any real desire for her but simply out of a desire springing from his earlier anger, but then hadn't she known that all along?

He was still looking at her, and continued to look at her for a long time, almost as though he was searching for something, she thought warily, and then at last he said coolly, 'Do you expect me to apologise?'

Jessica knew that he was challenging her to deny that she had enjoyed their lovemaking. Summoning her strength, she responded lightly, 'For your unwarranted accusations about my brother-in-law earlier, yes. For making love to me, no.'

She had a feeling that somehow she had angered him, without understanding why.

'You and he may not yet have been lovers, but that does not alter the fact that there's something between you,' he said curtly.

Jessica was about to tell him that she felt nothing but contempt for David, when totally unexpectedly he asked harshly, 'How long is it since you last made love?'

Every muscle in her body screamed a danger warning. There was just enough light for her to see that Lyle was frowning, and she knew it was pointless to lie; initially at least her body had been as unprepared for the masculinity of him as that of a totally inexperienced girl.

'Quite some time.' She didn't qualify her statement.

'So that response I got from you was based on physical frustration, was it?'

She wanted to scream at him that he was wrong, that she loved him, but pride and caution stopped her. Far better to let him think he was right. If she let him guess the truth she would lose him and the boys and the life she had here which she loved already. Logically she knew that it was unlikely that

he would ever come to feel about her the way she
did about him, but at least she would have…what?

'Well?'

His curt demand cut across her thoughts.

'I suppose it must have been.' How husky and
emotional her voice sounded; the voice of someone
in pain. Trying to sound flippant she added shakily,
'So now we know, frustration and anger make a
pretty lethal combination.'

To her surprise his only response was a smothered
curse, her mattress depressing as he got up and
pulled on his jeans, not looking at her as he picked
up his shirt and headed for the door. Once there he
paused, with his hand on the doorknob, his voice
harsh as he told her, 'Fortunately, it's a combination
we're not likely to repeat.'

And then he was gone, leaving her alone to dream
of how it could have been if instead of disliking her
he had loved her. She wouldn't be alone now. Instead she would be wrapped in his arms, listening
to his tender words of love and praise. Tears stung
her eyes and she buried her head into her pillow,
letting them fall.

THE NEXT FEW DAYS were purgatory. Jessica was
torn between the fear that Lyle would tell her he
wanted to end their marriage and the anguish
brought on by the fact that he was quite obviously
avoiding her. Even Stuart noticed it, commenting

that his father never seemed to spend any time with them in the evenings any more.

At least she had achieved a measure of success where the boys were concerned, Jessica consoled herself one afternoon as she worked in the garden. Both of them were much more open now; much more ready to accept Lyle as their father, and from the tiny scraps of information they had unwittingly given her, she had discovered that their withdrawal from him had been caused, not by their attachment to their mother, but by their realisation that she neither loved nor wanted them and their fear that Lyle would feel the same.

It was something she wanted to tell Lyle and discuss with him, but she was far too afraid to approach him. She dreaded seeing him look at her with contempt and dislike, or having him think that she was using the boys as an excuse to force on him an intimacy he plainly did not want.

In addition, nagging at her conscience and compounding her guilt was the very real fear that she could quite easily have conceived—it would be a week or more before she could know, but already she shuddered to think of Lyle's anger if she should discover that she had. There was quite simply no way he would want her to have his child, and yet knowing what she did about him, she knew he would never willingly consider an abortion, and neither was there any way she would want one, so that

left her with the painful knowledge that if she was
pregnant she would be inflicting upon him more
worries and responsibilities, and that it was quite
possible that he would allow the marriage to stand
simply because of the child.

From there it was only a short step to the acutely
unpalatable conviction that for a man who distrusted
the female sex as much as Lyle did it was all too
possible that he might conclude that she had deliberately engineered their lovemaking, intending to
become pregnant thus ensuring that he would be
forced to stand by their marriage and support her
and her child. He might even guess how she felt
about him, and suspect that she was using the child
as a form of moral blackmail.

All these thoughts and more surfaced far too fre-
quently for comfort, exhausting her emotionally and
physically, and even the garden had lost its normal
soothing effect on her senses. The boys were playing
on the lawn, but Jessica checked suddenly, noticing
the ominous silence. What on earth were they up to?

Putting down her trowel she headed in the direction of the lawn, coming to an abrupt and horrified
stop as she saw James standing looking up into the
branches of the ancient plum tree in the middle of
the lawn, while all that was visible of Stuart was his
legs, the rest of him cloaked in greenery.

It wasn't so much the fact that he had climbed
the tree that bothered her, but the knowledge that he

had done so in direct contravention of Lyle's wishes. The tree was old and dying, and he had already decided that in the winter it must come down because of its potential danger.

Even as she watched, Jessica heard the warning creak of the branch Stuart was sitting on. She heard James's frightened shout, his face white as he called out a warning to his brother, and then with a dry, rending sound the branch tore free of the trunk, both it and Stuart hurtling to the ground.

Jessica didn't remember running, but she must have done because she was there almost before the branch hit the ground, calling out anxiously to Stuart. He was lying among the foliage, his eyes closed, and his face white.

Beside her Jessica was aware of James's thin, keening cry as he sobbed hysterically. 'He's dead! Stuart's dead!'

Her stomach twisting in anguished knots, Jessica scrambled through the heavy leaves and small branches to reach the still figure of her stepson, not daring to move him as she bent over him, gently feeling for his pulse, trying to see if he was breathing.

It was only when she saw the even rise and fall of his chest that she was able to acknowledge how terrified she had been that James was right and Stuart had indeed been killed, but her relief was only short-lived. He might be alive, but he was still unconscious. Agonising twists of memory churned inside her, stories of children and adults for whom a blow on the head had resulted in a life that was no life at all, condemned to exist purely on a life-support machine.

She saw James scrambling towards her, reaching out to grab his brother's arm.

'No, don't touch him.'

She saw the younger boy's bottom lip tremble and wished she had not been so sharp, reaching out to comfort him as she explained. 'We don't know how badly hurt he is, James, so we mustn't move him. He isn't dead though.'

'I wish Dad was here.'

The young voice trembled and grew shrill and Jessica desperately shared his wish, but Lyle was out on his afternoon calls and wasn't due back for another couple of hours.

'You stay with Stuart,' she instructed, trying to appear calm, 'I'll go and ring for an ambulance.'

Over the telephone she explained what had happened as concisely as she could, and was told not to touch or move Stuart.

'We'll be with you just as soon as we can. Where are you again?' the cool controlled voice of the emergency operator asked.

Slowly Jessica gave the address, hearing curiosity sharpen the disembodied voice as the woman asked, 'You mean Dr Garnett's house?'

'Yes. Unfortunately my husband is out on call. I can ring him, but it would take him at least half an hour to get back and then there's the drive to the hospital.'

'Yes, you've done the right thing,' the other woman assured her. 'You can never tell with head injuries.'

The grave note in her voice only increased Jessica's fear, but fifteen minutes later, just as the ambulance pulled into the drive, Stuart opened his eyes.

Her breath totally suspended, Jessica waited for some reaction from him, and then to her relief his eyes cleared, his voice groggy but recognisable as he demanded shakily, 'What happened? My head hurts.'

'You fell out of the plum tree, my lad, that's what happened,' Jessica told him sternly. 'After your father had expressly forbidden you to climb it, too.'

'Dad!' Apprehension crossed the pale face. 'Is he here? Does he know?'

Before Jessica could reply she was having to move back to allow the ambulance crew to get to him.

'There doesn't seem to be any damage,' one of them told her, getting up from his knees. 'But we'll have to take him in for a check-up just to be on the safe side.'

'I'll follow you in my car,' Jessica suggested. 'I just want to leave a message for my husband first.'

She knew where Lyle would be and it didn't take her long to find the number of the farm. The farmer's mother-in-law who lived with them had severe diabetes which had resulted in ulceration of her legs. Lyle had gone out to check on her condition. The farmer's wife answered the phone, and when Jessica asked tersely to speak to Lyle, she went off immediately to get him.

'Jessica?'

Lyle's voice was sharp, with impatience, no doubt, Jessica thought tiredly, gripping the receiver with fingers that were hot and sticky. James was standing beside her, almost clinging to her, and she reached down to touch his shoulder in reassurance.

'Lyle, there's been an accident.' She had to raise her voice slightly to make herself heard above the static that had developed on the line.

'What? Are you all right?'

Amazed that he should automatically assume that she was the one who had been hurt, Jessica swallowed the painful lump in her throat. 'I'm fine,' she told him huskily. 'It's Stuart. He fell out…had a bad fall. He was unconscious for a while, but he came round just as the ambulance arrived. They've taken him in to hospital, Lyle, and James and I are going to follow him down there.'

She heard him say something, but the static was now so bad that she couldn't make out what it was.

Raising her voice again, she asked him if he had been able to hear her.

'Yes.' Miraculously the line cleared, allowing her to hear every terse nuance of his voice, but then it crackled again just as she heard him saying, 'I'll be there as soon as I can.'

'Is Dad going to the hospital too?' James asked anxiously when she had replaced the receiver.

He wanted his father to be there, Jessica saw, and her heart warmed a little. She smoothed the tousled dark hair so like his father's back off his forehead and said reassuringly, 'Yes, just as soon as he can.'

'Stuart will be all right, won't he?' James demanded as they drove to the hospital. 'He *will* be all right?'

Jessica smiled at him without committing herself; somehow she felt as though it might be bad luck to anticipate too optimistically, and so instead of replying she concentrated on her driving. Now that the first shock was over, she felt dreadfully weak and shaky, hardly fit to be in charge of a car. It would be the very last straw if she were to have an accident now. Fortunately they reached the hospital safely, hurrying into the casualty department where she gave her name to the nurse on duty.

'Ah yes, Stuart. He's been taken to the ward so that Mr Jeffries can examine him. Mr Jeffries is our Senior Consultant—luckily he happened to be with us today. If you'd like to go into the waiting-room.'

Jessica almost felt like screaming. She didn't want to go into the waiting-room at all, she wanted to go to Stuart, but before she could say so, the swing door opened violently and Lyle strode in.

'Daddy!' Tearing free of her James hurtled into his father's arms. Tears stung her eyes as Jessica watched the tender way Lyle bent towards his son, reassuring him.

He came over to her. 'Where's Stuart?'

'Mr Jeffries is examining him,' the nurse explained, overhearing. 'If you'd like to see him, Dr Garnett.'

For a moment Jessica thought she was going to be left alone while James and Lyle went to the ward, but then Lyle turned and said abruptly to her, 'Stuart will want to see you, I know. Will you come with us?'

Eagerly she hurried to his side, braving the nurse's frown of disapproval.

They found Stuart lying in a side ward, looking very small and vulnerable on the high white bed. A tall grey-haired man was bending over him. He straightened up when he saw Lyle and smiled.

'Nothing much wrong here,' he said reassuringly, 'just a large bump and an aching head.'

While Jessica hurried to Stuart's side, the consultant drew Lyle away slightly, and as she smiled down into Stuart's pale face Jessica could hear the faint hum of their conversation behind her. When it ceased she didn't immediately turn round.

'Your husband's gone to check up on one of his patients.' Mr Jeffries was standing beside her. 'I think you can go home now, young man,' he told Stuart, adding to Jessica, 'I can't see that there's any need to keep him in overnight. Even so you were right to call out the ambulance. He was lucky, he might easily not have been. Not that we're really equipped to perform brain surgery here, we would have had to take him to the special unit at Partington for that.' He shook his head regretfully and then stunned Jessica by saying, 'It's a pity your husband won't come back into surgery. He had all the makings of a very skilled neuro-surgeon. I had thought now that he was married that he might reconsider. Of course a consultant has to work very long hours.'

'So does a GP,' Jessica retorted indignantly, firing up at the implication that Lyle might have opted for the easier role in life.

Mr Jeffries laughed. 'Yes, yes, I know. But Lyle had a very special skill, and it grieves me to see him waste it. I take it that you would have no objection to his returning to surgery?'

Frowning, Jessica shook her head.

'Umm, I know how much it grieved him to give it up, but perhaps now...'

Would Lyle prefer to return to surgery? It was a

question that occupied much of Jessica's mind for the drive home.

James was in the car with her, Stuart travelling with Lyle where he would have more room. Although he was still subdued, his colour had been coming back by the time they left the hospital, and Jessica sent up a devout prayer of thanks that he had got off so lightly.

CHAPTER EIGHT

IN THE FIRST FEW DAYS after Stuart's accident, Jessica was kept far too busy to dwell too much on her own private feelings. Stuart had to be kept quiet for the first couple of days, and this had proved quite a challenge. What had surprised Jessica a little was that whenever Lyle was at home he willingly took over her nursing duties for her.

It was the first time she had been able to observe Lyle, the doctor, at close quarters, and she marvelled at his gentleness and patience. Coupled with a firmness which he exhibited whenever Stuart threatened to become frustrated with his enforced inactivity, he had a knack of soothing his son that she herself seemed unable to match.

Once, watching his tenderness with Stuart, she felt tears sting her eyes. This was the side of him she had known instinctively must exist but had never experienced. Nor ever would, she recognised drearily. Something in his relationship with Heather had sealed away any tenderness towards the female sex for ever. Now when she recalled Justine telling her how the much younger Lyle had placed his

young wife on a pedestal, adoring her almost
blindly, she felt sick with envy.

And then to cap it all, the morning that Lyle pro-
nounced that Stuart was fully fit, Jessica discovered
that she was not after all to have a child.

Until that moment she had not guessed how deep
had been her hope that she might. A child of Lyle's
to love and cherish as she would never be allowed
to love the father? Once she would have openly
mocked such sentimentality, but lately she had
changed. The love she had once denied could exist
was there, and she knew instinctively that it was no
mere sexual chemistry or infatuation she felt towards Lyle, but something that went far deeper and
would be with her all through her life.

What she had discovered from personal experience meant that she would have to amend large por-
tions of the outline for her new book, and when Lyle
had gone out on his morning calls she telephoned
her publishers in London to speak with her editor.

The conversation was a long one, but luckily her
editor had been very understanding about agreeing
to extending her earlier time limit. It would be impossible now for her to do any real work until after
the summer holidays when the boys would be back
at school.

She was going to miss their company once they
went back, but they needed the stimulus and com-
panionship of friends of their own age unless they

were to grow up solitary, and that was not what she wanted for them.

Andrea rang her during the afternoon, primarily to chat to her about the barbecue—how long ago that now seemed, Jessica thought wryly as she listened to her sister. She couldn't quite overcome her sense of guilt every time she saw Lyle, and she had taken to quietly slipping out of a room when he entered it, dreading to find herself alone with him and perhaps forced to listen to him saying that he now considered their marriage should end.

Lyle was no fool. He knew quite well that she was deliberately avoiding him, she had seen that in the cold and deliberate way his eyes challenged her, but it was a challenge she no longer had the heart to meet.

'One of the reasons I'm ringing is to ask you and Lyle to join us for dinner on Saturday evening,' Andrea told her, and then, as though sensing the refusal hovering on her sister's tongue, added coaxingly, 'please, Jess, the other guests will be colleagues of David's, and you know how much store he sets by having you as his sister-in-law. There's a senior lectureship coming up that he badly wants, and...'

'I honestly don't know if we'll be able to come, Andrea,' Jessica interrupted her sister. 'I'm not sure if Lyle will be free. I'll have to ring you back tomorrow and let you know.'

She had already decided that she wasn't going to

tell Lyle about the invitation. In her present vulnerable state it would be impossible for her to endure a full evening in his company without betraying herself, and the long drive to and from Andrea's would give him ample opportunity to bring up the subject of their marriage. Her face burned, even though she was alone, as it did every time she thought about her passionate response to him. It seemed impossible that he could not have guessed how she felt, but luckily he seemed to think that she had merely seen him as a substitute for David. Or perhaps that was what he wanted to believe.

The following morning she was downstairs later than usual. James had been sick during the night and when she went in to wake him up she had found him looking very pale and sorry for himself. Suspecting that too much half-ripened fruit from the garden was the culprit, she suggested that he stayed where he was until he was feeling a little better.

Lyle was standing by the kitchen table when she walked in, gulping down a mug of coffee. The work on the new kitchen was due to start the moment the boys were back at school, and much as Jessica longed for her new kitchen, she was dreading the upheaval.

'James is looking rather peaky,' she told him. 'Too many green apples, I suspect.'

'Umm, I'll go up and take a look at him. By the way, Andrea's phoned, and I've confirmed that we'll be able to make it on Saturday night. What's wrong?' he jeered, watching her face. 'Can't you stomach the thought of seeing Chalmers with your sister—his wife?' he reinforced before turning on his heel and heading for the hall.

It was just her luck that Andrea should have phoned while she was upstairs. Now there was no possibility of escaping from Saturday evening's dinner party—or from Lyle.

He was back downstairs almost immediately, confirming her own diagnosis of James's problem.

'Keep him in bed this morning. I should think he'll be well on the way to recovery by then.'

Lyle was proved right, and after a light lunch Jessica decided to take both boys into Oxford with her while she did some shopping. After the plum tree episode she had been reluctant to leave them alone for any length of time, and although both of them pulled faces at the thought of spending a sunny afternoon in the town, by the time she had driven there they were quite cheerful again.

After she had stowed away the food she had bought in the boot of her car, Jessica decided that it might be as well to buy something to wear for Andrea's dinner party. As a single woman she had attended a good many formal and semi-formal dinners following the publication of her books, and for these occasions she had purchased several severe and very plain dresses specifically designed to reinforce the fact that she was a psychologist first and a woman second, but for some reason as she mentally reviewed these outfits, none of them seemed suitable for Saturday evening.

Oxford had several excellent boutiques, and she found exactly what she was looking for in one of them, although at first the very striking colour combination of the silk suit, with its deep golden-yellow straight skirt, and mingled saffron, sapphire-blue and deep dark-pink toning top struck her as being a little too adventurous for her taste.

However, when she tried the outfit on, and saw how the straight skirt and nipped-in waistline of the jacket flattered her figure, she closed her mind against the unsuitability of such a very feminine outfit for a woman who had hitherto deliberately ignored any clothes that might enhance her female attributes.

Luckily the shop was able to provide a pair of high-heeled deep-saffron sandals to go with the suit, and less than half an hour after walking into it Jessica was walking out again, carrying her parcels.

'I liked you in it,' Stuart commented as they headed back to the car. He seemed to think for a moment and then added, 'It made me think of a hot sunny day.'

Jessica glanced at his down-bent head, thinking again how very artistic and sensitive Lyle's elder son was. Once she would have assumed those traits came from his mother, but now she was not so sure. Lyle had displayed a core of sensitivity she had not expected, at least where his patients were concerned.

'Yes. It made your hair look all pretty and shiny,' James added stoutly, not to be outdone.

When they got home Jessica hung the suit carefully in her wardrobe so that any creases could drop out.

The decorations were now almost complete. Next week the new carpets would arrive and so would the covers she had had made for the furniture and the curtains.

It was frightening how quickly she had come to think of this house as 'home', too quickly, perhaps...

By Saturday she was in a state of tense nervousness, glad that Lyle had been called out during the afternoon, and half hoping that the emergency would mean that they would not be able to attend Andrea's dinner party; but she heard Lyle's car in the drive, just as she was giving the boys their evening meal.

A babysitter hadn't been difficult to arrange. Lyle's receptionist had a niece at home from university for the holidays who had gladly accepted the opportunity to earn a little extra money, and her father had arranged to drop her off half an hour before they were due to leave.

Lyle came into the kitchen, pausing to ruffle both

boys' hair. Stuart grinned back at him, all his previous truculence and reserve gone. If she had achieved nothing else at least she had given him this, Jessica thought, absorbed in the very normality of the small domestic scene.

'What time are we due at Andrea's?' Lyle asked her, helping himself to one of the scones she had baked for the boys.

'Half-past eight.'

She saw him glance at his watch, her stomach cramping distressingly at the sight of his sinewy brown arm. It was ridiculous that something as mundane as seeing a man glance at his watch should affect her so tormentingly; something she herself would have openly scoffed at had someone else related it to her, and yet here she was gripped by an almost feverish need to reach out and touch him.

'Jessica, are you all right?'

Confusion momentarily shadowed her eyes at his sharply incisive tone. 'Yes, yes, I'm fine.'

If only that were true, Jessica thought, hurriedly turning her back to him and busying herself pouring the boys glasses of homemade lemonade, but she was feeling far from fine. With a small shock she realised that for the last two days she had barely eaten a thing. Her appetite seemed to have totally deserted her since that fateful stormy night when she and Lyle had made love, but the tension growing inside her since Lyle's announcement about tonight's dinner had destroyed what small appetite she had had.

'You look pale.'

Jessica heard the door into the hall open and released a shaky breath only to feel increased tremors of apprehension grip her when Lyle returned only seconds later, with a glass of brandy.

'Here, drink this,' he instructed her. 'You look as though you need it.'

She wanted to refuse, but he was looking at her as though he would pour the spirit down her throat by force if she refused. She had seldom seen him look so angry since that first fateful encounter. The sympathy she had seen him exhibit towards the children when they felt off-colour was plainly not going to be forthcoming in her case.

He was still frowning at her as she took the glass from him. 'Are you sure there's nothing wrong?'

He was looking at her watchfully, and suddenly Jessica realised what was in his mind. As she had done, he was obviously thinking that she could have conceived his child, and was just as obviously not at all pleased at the thought.

Her own eyes hardening, Jessica took the glass from him and swallowed its contents. She wasn't a drinker and the effect of the undiluted spirit on her stomach was immediate.

'I'm perfectly well,' she told him curtly, turning away from him to put the glass on the table, almost hating him for letting her see how little he relished the thought that she might be carrying his child.

It was doubly hurtful to remember Justine telling her how he had refused to allow Heather an abortion; no doubt in her case, had she been pregnant... Tears stung her eyes which she tried to deceive herself were the result of the undiluted brandy.

'I'll go up and shower now so that the bathroom's free for you,' she heard Lyle saying behind her, and surely it could only be the brandy that tormented her to point out to him that as a man and wife they could surely share the bathroom, but fortunately caution made her hold back the words and keep silent.

She heard the babysitter arrive while she was upstairs putting the finishing touches to her make-up. Lyle answered the door and Jessica hurried downstairs to introduce herself to Susan and her father.

She sensed from the firm handshake she received from the latter that part of his purpose in bringing his daughter round himself had been to assure himself as to their suitability to employ her, and Jessica felt herself warming to such a concerned parent.

After refusing the drink Lyle offered, he excused himself, suggesting that he call to pick Susan up at one o'clock.

She had two younger brothers, Susan explained to Jessica as she introduced her to the boys, and indeed her manner towards them was friendly but firm.

'That's a lovely outfit you're wearing,' she complimented Jessica shyly.

'Indeed it is.'

Jessica hadn't heard Lyle come into the room, her nerve-endings jumping tensely as she registered his soft compliment. It would be foolish to place any importance on it. Quite obviously he was simply playing the devoted husband for Susan's benefit. Smiling tautly at the younger girl, Jessica picked up her bag and headed for the door, leaving Lyle to follow her.

'Do you want to drive or shall I?'

They were going in her car, and Jessica checked, slightly surprised. 'I think I'd prefer to be a passenger,' she told him. 'This skirt is all too prone to crease.'

'Mmm, silk, isn't it?' He reached out and took the fabric of her jacket between his thumb and finger, standing so close to her that she was immediately aware of the heat of his body. It took every ounce of willpower she possessed not to melt against him and beg him to take her in his arms.

Shaken by the violence of her feelings, Jessica stepped back, forgetting how high her heels were and stumbling slightly on the uneven drive. Instantly Lyle steadied her, his fingers curling round her arm, making her shiver in responsive delight.

'Cold?' He was frowning as he watched her, and

Jessica knew why. It was a hot August night with
no reason on earth why she should be feeling cold.

'No, just fright. I thought I was going to fall for
a moment.'

Fortunately he seemed to accept her explanation,
releasing her immediately and walking over to the
car to unlock the passenger door for her.

Her fear that once they were alone Lyle might
bring up the subject of their marriage subsided a
little when he made no attempt to speak, instead
feeding a cassette into the machine, flooding the car
with some of her favourite chamber music.

The journey seemed to last for ever, but eventually they were there, Andrea coming out to welcome
them, laughing slightly as her 'bulge' got in the way
as she hugged Jessica.

'Just you wait until it's your turn,' she threatened
teasingly when Jessica laughed.

Beside her Lyle tensed, and as easily as though
she could read his mind Jessica knew what he was
thinking. It was impossible to stop the faint touch
of scorn edging up into her voice as she responded
coolly to her sister's teasing.

'Well, it most definitely isn't on the cards at the
moment.'

Although it was Andrea she addressed her comment to, it was meant for Lyle, but conversely instead of making him relax it only seemed to increase
his tension.

'Come on inside and meet the others.'

Andrea had a new glow and self-confidence about her that had restored much of the spiritedness she seemed to have lost recently. Jessica noticed that she seemed far less inclined to cling to David, her manner assured and calm.

There were three other couples in the drawing-room; all the men were David's colleagues, and Jessica recognised two of them as senior lecturers, no doubt invited so that David could indulge in some discreet lobbying, Jessica reflected wryly.

This aspect of the academic scene had never appealed to her; quite the reverse, and although she made no protest when David paraded her in front of his superiors, almost as though she were a prize exhibit in some sort of show, the gleam in her eyes should have warned him that she didn't appreciate being used to further his career.

'Jessica is shortly to submit another book to her publishers,' David told them, smiling at her. 'This time I believe the subject is "Love and its effect on Western Culture".'

Jessica was all too glad to escape on the pretext of giving Andrea a hand in the kitchen. As she tugged her arm away from David's too-tight grip she noticed that Lyle was already deep in conversation with the wives of David's colleagues; one of them, a particularly attractive woman in her late thirties, was standing so close to him that their bodies touched. Far from moving away whenever she came near him, Lyle seemed to be enjoying the light physical contact. The woman turned towards him, touching his arm in emphasis of some point she was making, and Jessica swallowed hard as she saw the way Lyle looked down into her animated face, jealousy seizing her body in a paralysing grip.

'Jessica?'

Andrea was looking at her curiously. 'Anything wrong?'

'No.'

'Umm, you look as though you need a strong drink. Have this, David made it for me.' She grimaced faintly. 'He seems to forget that in my present condition alcohol isn't a good idea.'

Automatically Jessica took the glass her sister proffered, downing the contents quickly.

Andrea's eyebrows rose. 'My goodness, things *have* changed,' she marvelled. 'I've never seen you do that before.'

The gin and tonic had been far stronger than Jessica expected, hitting her stomach so explosively that she had to lean against the wall momentarily as she followed Andrea into the kitchen.

'Everything's organised,' Andrea told her. 'This hot weather is an ideal excuse not to bother with any complicated menus. I've done a cheese soufflé to start with, and provided we get everyone sitting down at the right time there won't be any problems there. David bought me a new ice-cream-maker a couple of weeks ago, so I've experimented with lemon sorbet before the main course—salmon baked in herbs and a selection of vegetables, and then homemade ice-cream with fruit for dessert, plus a cheeseboard. David's got in some vintage port that ought to go down well with the professors, or so he hopes.'

There was enough satirical indulgence in her sister's voice for Jessica to glance at her rather sharply.

'Oh, it's all right, it's just that since your marriage I've come to realise that David isn't the God he'd like me to believe. Frankly, Jess, I feel far more comfortable now that I realise that he's human just like everyone else. I don't feel that I have to try as hard for one thing.' She fiddled with some plates, her back to Jessica as she said wryly, 'I think I knew all the time that you weren't interested in him, but I wouldn't admit the truth to myself. I used you as a defence mechanism, I suppose. Our marriage may not be ideal but so far it has worked, and I intend to see that it goes on working.'

If her sister continued to behave in this new, more spirited, determined fashion Jessica suspected that it probably would, although it would not have been a situation she could have lived with happily. David would continue to be unfaithful to her, and Andrea must know that.

'Would you go through and herd them all into the

dining-room? I think the soufflé's just about ready.
I've put place cards out,' she pulled a face. 'Personally I thought it was a bit stuffy, but David wants
to make an impression.'

Going back into the drawing-room Jessica caught
David's eye as she moved towards him. He was already pouring out a fresh drink for the man standing
with him, and automatically started to pour one for
Jessica.

'G and T for you, and don't refuse, I saw you
gulping down your last one. Not like you, Jess. Not
suffering from the strain of marriage already, are
you?' He laughed at his own wit, causing Jessica to
grit her teeth and accept the full glass he gave her.

'Andrea wants everyone to sit down. The soufflé
is just about ready.'

Leaving David to organise the male guests, Jessica hurried over to Lyle who was still talking to the
women.

'My dear, your husband is the most fascinating
man,' the oldest of the trio commented to Jessica,
smiling at her. 'But then I must confess that we do
have an interest in common. I practised as a GP
myself for several years before I married. Alas, being the wife of an academic is something of a full-
time activity, and so reluctantly I had to give up my
career when the children came along.'

'Personally I find doctors the most fascinating
men,' the blonde standing next to Lyle said softly.

'Perhaps it's because they have such an insight into the feminine mystique.'

Jessica had a childish impulse to say something extremely rude. It was plain to see that the woman was trying to strike up a flirtation with Lyle, while he, damn him, was doing absolutely nothing to discourage her—far from it! Where was the austere coldness she was so accustomed to?

'Oh good,' Janet Holmes cooed enthusiastically to Lyle when they went into the dining-room. 'I'm sitting next to you.'

It was ridiculous for a woman of nearly forty to behave in such an obvious way, Jessica thought nastily, sitting down next to Lyle. She was still holding the drink David had given her, and rather than disturb Andrea's carefully organised table, she emptied her glass quickly, hurriedly disposing of it on a nearby small table.

It was only as she sat down that she realised how strong the drink was, and how potentially dangerous on an empty stomach. She could see Lyle frowning slightly at her, but strangely that no longer seemed to matter. Instead she was conscious of a pleasurable haze that seemed to grow rather than decrease as she toyed with Andrea's rich cheese soufflé, and drank two glasses of deliciously chill white wine.

It was when Andrea was serving the salmon that Lyle bent towards her and murmured curtly, 'I suggest you don't have anything more to drink.'

David was already on his way round the table with a fresh bottle of wine—chosen especially to complement the salmon, she heard him saying to Janet Holmes. Lyle had not suggested that *she* had had too much to drink, Jessica thought bitterly, and the other woman had consumed as much as she had herself.

Who was Lyle anyway to tell her what she might and might not do? Wilfully she allowed David to fill her glass, even raising it mockingly in Lyle's direction before taking a sip. The evening was beginning to take on a relaxed glow she had never expected; indeed she could not remember when she had last felt this relaxed about anything. If only this underlying feeling of tension would go away, though.

But it didn't, continuing to linger through the delicious ice-cream sweet and the cheese and biscuits which Andrea insisted she had, pointing out that the Roquefort cheese had been chosen especially with her in mind.

Of course it was impossible to refuse the glass of port David had poured for her, even though it did take a certain amount of owlish concentration for her to be able to lift the glass to her lips without spilling any of it.

Afterwards while they drank coffee and ate petits fours in the drawing-room, Jessica found that she still had a full glass of port.

As she blinked and studied it David said smoothly, 'Oh come on, Jess, we might as well finish it off.'

He seemed amused about something, almost maliciously so, but Jessica had had far too much to drink to analyse what.

Having told her once that he thought she had had enough to drink Lyle had almost totally ignored her, allowing himself to be almost completely monopolised by Janet Holmes.

What was it the other woman had that she did not? Jessica wondered bitterly; and she certainly must have something, because Lyle had barely taken his eyes off her. Even Andrea noticed it because she paused once to bend down and murmur apologetically to her, 'Sorry about Janet flirting with Lyle, but she's that sort of woman, I'm afraid.'

For once Jessica did not repudiate David when he came and sat next to her. He wanted to talk to her about her book but Jessica fobbed him off, conscious that she was going to have to do some major re-writes on it. She could not now in all honesty dismiss the power of 'love' as radically as she had done before.

'How's the experiment working, then?' David asked her, looking at Lyle. His words penetrated her tipsy fog, reminding Jessica of the claim she had made when she told him she was marrying Lyle. God, how David would laugh if he knew the truth!

That she had fallen in love with a man who totally repudiated her.

Her face felt stiff as she forced a smile, and said lightly, 'So far, very well. It's given me a new insight into the whole question of marriage. I've certainly managed to get quite a lot of information for my book from it.'

It was pride and pride alone that motivated her words, and Lyle was too far away to have heard them. She saw David smile and alarm feathered warningly down her spine. She had drunk far too much, and unless she was careful she could easily be very indiscreet.

'I take it he still doesn't know exactly why you married him?' David asked her.

Jessica shook her head, and then wished she hadn't as it spun uncomfortably.

She could see Lyle coming towards her, and apprehension cramped her stomach. Andrea was with him, and it gave Jessica a disconcerting sensation in her midriff to have him standing over her looking down at her, as though somehow she was an errant child rather than an adult.

'I think we'd better leave.'

He was talking to Andrea and not herself, but Jessica felt the words were intended for her.

'Oh, surely not yet. Let me get you both a nightcap.' That was David, smiling gleefully at some apparently private joke.

'I think not.' Lyle sounded both curt and remote. 'I'm driving,' he pointed out to David, 'and I've seen far too many accidents caused by drivers under the influence of alcohol to want to drive over the limit myself.'

'But what about Jess? She isn't driving.'

'No, I think Jessica's already had enough.'

She wanted to protest that he had no right to treat her like a child, to make such decisions for her, but somehow his hand was under her elbow and forcing her to her feet, and she was walking into the hall with Andrea clucking anxiously at her side.

'Oh dear,' she heard her sister say through the fog threatening to engulf her, 'I don't know what's come over Jess tonight. She hardly ever drinks.'

Of the drive back to Sutton Parva Jessica only retained fleeting and very brief memories. She fell asleep almost the moment she got into the car, waking occasionally, and having to be shaken awake by Lyle once they were actually home.

She tried to get out of the car and suddenly found her legs as awkward and unstable as those of a newborn colt.

Above her she heard Lyle swear and then suddenly she was in his arms and being carried into the hall and upstairs.

In her room, he dropped her unceremoniously on the bed and then stood back to look grimly at her.

'I'll talk to you once Susan's gone,' he told her

abruptly. 'Somehow I don't think her father would retain any good impression of us if he could see you in this state.'

There had been more irony in his voice than disgust, but even so Jessica was vividly conscious of how unappealing she must appear. There was nothing more off-putting, surely, than a drunken woman, and if she was not drunk then she was certainly very, very tipsy.

She got off the bed, alarmed by the way the room swung round her, and slowly made her way to the bathroom. Downstairs she could hear voices, and guessed that Susan's father had arrived to collect his daughter.

In the bathroom she shed her clothes and stood under the shower, shivering under the cold water, telling herself that she deserved this self-inflicted icy torture.

It helped to clear her head a little, but her body still felt as boneless as cotton wool, her balance unstable and her legs unresponsive. She managed to get out of the shower and suddenly shocked herself by the way she started to tremble, her teeth chattering together, as she tried feverishly to make her way to the other side of the bathroom and the protective warmth of a towel.

She heard Lyle come upstairs and then call her name, presumably having discovered that she was not in her room.

The next moment the bathroom door burst open and he stormed in, coming to an abrupt halt as he surveyed her damp, shivering frame.

'What the...?'

'I thought a cold shower might sober me up,' Jessica explained, her teeth chattering so much she could barely speak.

Her whole body seemed to be in the grip of a shivering ague now, so much so that she daren't let go of the side of the shower.

Lyle cursed again, reaching for a towel then coming towards her. 'You crazy fool,' she heard him storm furiously. 'Don't you realise the shock to your system of a cold shower on a hot night like this, especially on top of all that alcohol? Come here.'

Somehow he managed to envelop her in the towel and detach her tightly curled fingers from the shower, at the same time picking her up in his arms as easily as though she were James's weight.

He carried her through into her own room, sitting down on her bed with her on his lap, briskly rubbing her freezing body with the thick towel.

Slowly the shivers stopped, the icy chill in her body replaced by a languorous, dangerous heat which she instantly recognised.

Miraculously now her head was completely clear. What on earth had possessed her to go on drinking after Lyle had warned her not to? Heavens, surely she could have realised for herself what she was doing? She had always assiduously avoided alcohol in the past, carefully monitoring what she drank, but tonight for some reason… No, not for some nebulous, half-understood reason at all. She knew exactly why she had drunk so much: initially it had been because she had been so terrified that Lyle might make use of the fact that they were alone to tell her he wanted to end their marriage, and then because she had been totally unable to endure the sight of him with Janet Holmes.

'All right now?'

He had stopped touching her now, his hands lightly resting on her waist, ready to put her away from him and leave her room, she recognised miserably. If only he would stay with her. If only there were some way; her breath caught in her throat, her body hurting as she recognised his desire to get away from her.

'Lyle…'

She looked up at him, watching the guarded shadows hide whatever lay in his eyes.

Her fingers fluttered against his skin, stroking the taut line of his jaw in a gesture both pleading and helpless.

'Please don't go. Please stay with me.'

Part of her was horrified at what she was saying, what she was doing, but she was overwhelmed by a surge of despair as his hands moved from her waist to her arms, ready to thrust her off, and without even thinking properly, she clung to him, pressing her mouth to his, and kissing him with a defiant, desperate hunger, not knowing and certainly not caring that the towel had fallen away from her upper body and that her breasts were pressed damply against the front of Lyle's shirt.

She could feel the pressure of his fingers as they locked round her wrists, but strangely he did not push her away, his mouth suddenly relaxing under her own, his hand going from her wrist to the back of her head, where his fingers wove into her hair and pressed against her scalp, his lips moving on hers as he muttered rawly against them, 'My God, I didn't want this, but you make it impossible for me to refuse.'

CHAPTER NINE

SHE WAS IN HEAVEN, Jessica thought achingly,
drowning in the unexpected delight of having Lyle's
mouth against her own, his harsh unrhythmic
breathing telling its own story as his hands swept
her body with a fierce compulsion, pushing away
the towel, cupping her breasts so that his mouth
could savour the pulsating fulness of first one and
then the other breast.

Reality slid away from her as easily as she shed
the towel, everything else blurring into insignifi-
cance as she felt her body become an eager slave of
the desire Lyle aroused within her. Beneath his
hands her body arched, instituting a delicate dance
of delirium, her own fingers eager if somewhat
clumsy as she tugged at the buttons of his shirt, shivering in open pleasure as they gave way to allow
her access to his body.

She felt him shudder as she touched his skin, tiny
shivers of responsive awareness creating a frisson of
arousal within her body as she moved wantonly
against him, hearing him gasp and mutter something
incomprehensible against her ear as her teeth caught

against a hard male nipple. She touched it with her tongue, teasingly, testing his reaction, shuddering herself when his fingers tangled in her hair and tightened in mute recognition of the effect she had on him. His thumb brushed the delicate skin behind her ear, his tongue searching its curves with deliberate eroticism.

She felt her response to his touch all the way down to her toes which curled in automatic reflex. Her body felt weightless, languorous, her mind completely cast adrift as she shed the inhibitions she had always wrapped so protectively around herself.

It was her purpose and her pleasure to arouse Lyle to the point where like her nothing mattered more than desire. Already he wanted her; his body hard and urgent against her own, his mouth burning her skin where it touched it.

She found the zip of his trousers, and slid it down, feeling the tension in his body as her nails accidentally scraped against his flesh. He shuddered violently, trapping her hand against his body, his mouth burning into the tender flesh of her throat, searching for the frantic pulse that beat there.

Waves of dizziness spread through her, heat engulfing her body as she tipped her head back under the pressure of his mouth, not sure if the heavy hammer-blows she could feel came from his heart or her own.

She wanted him and she wanted him now, her

body moving frenziedly against his, accepting the intimate caress of his fingers with spasmodic delight. She was lying on the bed now, breathing erratically beneath his caress, shocked into an anguished protest when he suddenly withdrew from her, leaving her tense and aching with the desire he had aroused. She sat up, shivering slightly as reality impinged on her erotic dream, but Lyle was simply removing the rest of his clothes.

When he came back to her, he didn't speak, simply staring down at her, absorbing every minute detail of her aroused, naked body. And then he was on the bed, his mouth and hands caressing and arousing every millimetre of sensitive skin until she was crying out incoherently for him to finish it.

As if he knew exactly when she reached the fine line dividing desire from torment he moved over her, her body arching eagerly to receive the weight of his, the first slow thrust of his body within her own wrenching from him a low hoarse cry which penetrated her own aching desire, doubling her pleasure in his possession when she knew how much he too had craved it.

It was over too quickly, the tense spiralling delight exploding inside her almost before she had time to register its onset. She felt Lyle reach his climax and knew a primitive delight as she felt him deep within her while her body still quivered in the aftermath of its own release.

He slumped over her, his skin hot and damp with sweat, his breathing harshly irregular. Not wanting to let him go, Jessica wrapped her arms round him, pressing her mouth to the salty heat of his throat, letting her senses absorb the maleness of him. She felt tired, so very tired...

'JESSICA, ARE YOU AWAKE yet?'

James's faintly accusatory voice penetrated her light sleep. As she opened her eyes Jessica glanced at her watch, horrified to see that it was gone nine. Heavens, she must have slept like a log. Her body ached, her mouth felt dry and faintly sour with the residue of last night's alcohol, although mercifully she had no headache. Suddenly her body tensed as certain memories began to surface and refused to go away. She closed her eyes, feeling her skin go hot. Dear God, last night she had virtually seduced Lyle. Her body crawled with shame and anguish. Why on *earth* hadn't he stopped her? Her mouth twisted slightly. Why should she expect him to be any more impervious to desire than she was herself? It would be only natural for him to be in an aroused state after all Janet's determined flirting. She shuddered to think of her body being used as a substitute for that of the other woman, her eyes suddenly dry and gritty.

'Jessica?'

James was beside her bed now, looking down at

her with a small frown. 'Dad said I wasn't to disturb you, but Stuart and I are hungry, and Dad's had to go out on an emergency call.'

'I'm getting up now,' Jessica told him, knowing that it was pointless staying in bed any longer. At least she didn't have to face Lyle immediately, although what on earth she was going to say to explain her behaviour when she did see him, she had no idea.

In the end, even though she castigated herself mentally for being a coward, she decided that her best course of action was simply to let Lyle raise the subject if he wished to. She shivered a little. If he raised it? Surely he was bound to do so? After all he had been very definite when he stated the rules of their marriage, and on this occasion she had most definitely been the one to break them.

He came into the kitchen while she was washing up the breakfast dishes. Both boys were in the garden, and although she had heard his car she had resolutely kept her back to the door, not knowing how much she might betray if she had to face him.

As he opened the door, her throat suddenly went dry with apprehension and she ran the cold tap, filling a glass and then sipping the cold water.

'Hangover?'

He was standing right behind her, and Jessica winced at the harsh sound of his voice. He had every reason to sound condemnatory, and it was quite ridiculous for her to wish that he would take her in his arms and tell her that he loved her—ridiculous and impossible.

Without turning she shook her head, and then mumbled, 'Not that I don't deserve one.' Her face was hot as she remembered how much she had drunk the previous night, and how she had behaved when he tried to stop her.

Silence greeted her remark. Keeping her back to him Jessica took a deep breath and fibbed, 'I'm afraid I can't remember much about last night at all.'

She could feel the tension gripping her, the sick knowledge that for the first time in her life she had told a deliberate lie, but she could simply not stand there in torment any longer waiting for the blow to fall. Now she had given him the ideal opportunity to tell her in no uncertain terms exactly what had happened, but to her stunned disbelief she felt him move slightly away from her, the legs of one of the kitchen chairs scraping across the floor as he pulled it out from the table and sat down.

His silence forced her to turn round and look at him. He was frowning slightly, his face drawn and tired; guilt and love twisted painfully inside her. She wanted to go to him and beg him to understand why she had behaved as she had, but fear stopped her. Now she knew exactly why Andrea had preferred to believe that David was having an affair with her rather than someone else; why her sister continued in her marriage even though she knew her husband to be unfaithful. Now at last she understood how crippling this emotion called love could be.

She waited tensely for Lyle to speak, to tell her that she had broken their agreement, but instead all he said was, 'Mmm, I gathered you weren't used to consuming that amount of alcohol, which leads me to wonder why you did.'

He was looking at her now, and there was no way she could drag her gaze from his. His mouth widened in a parody of a smile, his voice chillingly disdainful as he added, 'The strain of seeing your lover with your sister, perhaps?'

After everything that had happened did he still believe she loved David? Jessica clutched at the excuse he had thrown her, unable to believe that he had not guessed the truth. Without answering his taunt she set about making some coffee, and as though he had not really expected any answer to his question, Lyle began to look through the papers.

The ordeal was over, Lyle was not going to bring up the subject of last night. Perhaps he thought that she genuinely did not remember what had happened. Perhaps he felt that he himself was in some part to blame for giving way to his own physical needs. Perhaps because of the boys he did not want to set aside their marriage. She had after all established a good bond with them, and that had been the main reason he had married her.

She should have felt happy and relieved that nothing was going to be said, but instead, ridiculously, she found herself wishing that he would say something; that he would at least acknowledge the fact that they had been lovers, and not simply ignore the event as though it had never happened; as though it was so unimportant that it was not even worth remembering or discussing.

CHAPTER TEN

A WEEK AFTER Andrea's dinner party, Justine called and unwittingly confirmed Jessica's own view as to why Lyle had made no mention of what had happened that night.

She and Jessica were sitting in the kitchen drinking coffee, and keeping an eye on the three boys, who were playing on the lawn on their bikes. Peter had just had a birthday, and had brought his brand new BMX round to show his cousins. The earlier antipathy which had existed between them had now gone, and noting this Justine said affectionately to Jessica, 'It's all your doing, you know. You've given them so much, Jess. Sometimes when I look at them now I can't believe the difference you've made in their lives. It's shattering, really, to realise what a difference genuine love and caring mean to a child.'

'They were loved before I came along,' Jessica reminded her abruptly. 'Lyle loved them.'

'Yes, I know, but they couldn't communicate with one another, could they: Lyle was still suffering from his guilt about Heather's death—not that I believe he should have blamed himself. She always was impetuous and selfish, but the fact that he did feel guilty, that because of Heather he had seen so little of the boys, created a wall between them. I must say it's rather nice for once to know that I was right and my dear brother was wrong. He never wanted...'

She broke off, colouring slightly, but Jessica merely gave her a bright smile and said as cheerfully as she could, 'Oh, it's all right, Jus, I know he didn't want to marry me—at least not at first.'

'Maybe so, but I can't believe there's any doubt in his mind now about the success of your marriage. The boys adore you, and Lyle himself looks so much more relaxed. The pair of you fit well together, Jess.'

'Our marriage is a business arrangement and nothing more,' Jessica felt bound to point out to the other woman, while wondering if perhaps Justine had just given her Lyle's reason for not bringing up the matter of her tipsy seduction of him: namely that he didn't want to prejudice their relationship because of his sons.

'I know it started off that way,' Justine agreed, 'but I don't think you're anywhere near as indifferent to him as you pretend, Jess, nor him to you. I've seen you together,' she continued before Jessica could interrupt. 'Oh, I know Lyle doesn't give much away! Heather hurt him badly, but that was his own fault. Anyone could have seen how selfish she was, but Lyle chose not to, and instead put her on a pedestal. I've been telling him for years that just because one woman let him down that's no reason to condemn the entire female sex.'

'Love isn't something that can be cut off at will,' Jessica pointed out to her. 'If Lyle still loves Heather...'

'Loves her?' Justine looked stunned. 'Good God, whatever gave you that idea? By the time they were divorced Lyle well and truly despised her. Initially he tried to persuade her to keep the marriage going because of the boys, but she told him she couldn't care less about them, and that if she'd had her way she'd never have given birth to them. She was bitter because she had had to abandon her own medical training half way through, bitter and jealous of Lyle's success, and so she told him she was going to keep the boys and that he had to support all three of them so that she could go back to her studies.

'Of course Lyle gave in to her, for the boys' sake, not hers, and then the moment she was qualified she told him she was going abroad to work and that she intended dumping the kids on him. He told me after her accident that he felt if he hadn't lost his temper with her she wouldn't have run off and had that accident, but equally if she hadn't gone to him and forced the confrontation on him, he wouldn't have lost his temper.' Justine shrugged. 'It was a tragic accident, but an accident nonetheless.' She paused and frowned as she looked at Jessica. 'Did you *really* think he still loved Heather?'

Jessica felt trapped, but it was pointless to lie. 'Yes, I did,' she confirmed.

'Mmm, and now that you know he doesn't...'

She knew what Justine was getting at, but she shook her head decisively. 'It makes no difference, Justine,' she told her firmly. 'Lyle may not still love Heather, but believe me, he feels nothing for me.'

'If you say so.' Justine grinned at her, and somehow Jessica did not think her sister-in-law was convinced.

After Justine and Peter had gone their conversation lingered in Jessica's thoughts. Justine had soon guessed at her own feelings, but then Justine liked playing *deus ex machina,* as she had proved by the way she had forced Lyle into marrying her in the first place. Couldn't it be that, guessing how she felt about him, Justine was now trying to encourage her to believe her feelings might be returned so that she would perhaps approach Lyle?

Justine liked and approved of her, she had said as much, and practical woman that she was, no doubt she felt that the future of their marriage would be much more secure if it changed from a business arrangement to one with a more normal basis. Of course Justine was not to know that they had already been lovers, and that far from improving their marriage, it had only widened the gap between them.

No, she would not fall into the trap of believing that Justine might be right and that Lyle might actually care for her as a person. It would be the height of self-delusion to do so, especially when she knew the truth!

Two days after Justine's visit, Jessica received a frightened phone call from her sister.

'Jess, can you come over straight away?' Andrea begged. 'I went for my check-up this morning and Dr Ford wasn't too happy with my blood pressure. He wants to get me into hospital for a couple of days until it comes down, but there's no one to look after William. I can't reach David. He's in a meeting and it's likely to go on for some hours yet. If you could just come over and take William home with you...'

Quickly reassuring her sister that she would be there as quickly as possible, Jessica then rang Justine and asked her if she could drop James and Stuart off on her way to her sister's.

'I'm not sure what state Andrea will be in. I might have to run her to hospital and stay there for a while, I don't know. If you could just keep an eye on them for me until I get back with William?'

'Of course I will,' Justine confirmed immediately. 'Bring them over when you're ready.'

It didn't take long for Jessica to explain to the

boys what had happened. Neither of them showed the slightest resentment at having to spend the day with Justine, both of them secure enough in her love now to know that they were not being passed over in favour of William. Scribbling a note for Lyle, whom she was expecting back for lunch, Jessica bundled the boys into the car and set off for Justine's.

Knowing the urgency involved Justine did not press her to stop for coffee, running out to the car to help the boys out and telling Jessica not to worry about them. Jessica hugged them both before backing out of the drive and continuing on her journey to her sister's.

As she had half expected she found Andrea in a semi-hysterical state, a fact which could hardly do her high blood pressure any good, Jessica thought worriedly, as she coaxed her into sitting down and putting her feet up, while she assured Andrea that William was more than welcome to stay with her just as long as was needed.

'I don't think it will come to that,' Andrea told her fretfully. 'David will be home later, and he has some holidays owing to him that he could take. If only I knew how long they'll keep me in!'

'Well, the more you worry about that, the longer it will be,' Jessica warned her firmly. 'Are they sending an ambulance for you or shall I take you in?'

'Dr Ford's going to ring me just as soon as he's made all the arrangements.'

As though on cue the phone rang, and Jessica went to answer it. Andrea's doctor sounded relieved that there was someone with her, and gratefully accepted Jessica's suggestion that she drive her sister to hospital.

'If you could that would be marvellous,' he confirmed. 'I don't really care for the idea of her driving herself. I'll be there to meet her. I've got some other patients to visit there.'

It was Jessica who packed Andrea's small case and checked that her sister had everything she might need for her stay. They were half way to the hospital when Andrea suddenly gripped Jessica's wrist, her eyes dilating with anguish as she cried, 'Jess, I don't want to lose my baby. I'm so frightened.'

'I don't think there's the slightest question of that,' Jessica told her firmly, hoping she was right. 'The best thing you can do, Andrea, is to try and relax a little, give your blood pressure a chance to come down.' As she spoke she glanced warningly towards the back of the car to remind Andrea that William was there, and could well be frightened by what his mother was saying.

Fortunately by the time they reached the hospital Andrea seemed to have calmed down a little.

Her doctor, Dr Ford, was a pleasant, authoritative

man with a tired smile and a shock of iron-grey hair, his manner both soothing and firm.

Jessica waited with William while they got Andrea settled, and then approached Dr Ford when he came to find them, asking how Andrea was.

'Comfortable. I think we've got her in time— No, there's no question of her losing the baby,' he confirmed in answer to Jessica's question. 'At least not if she does as she's told.'

'I'm going to stay with William until his father comes home,' Jessica told the doctor. 'Do you know how long she'll be in here?'

'That depends very much on how sensibly she behaves,' she was told, confirming her own views on Andrea's condition.

As might have been expected William was very subdued on the drive back to Andrea's house, blurting out worriedly as Jessica stopped the car in the drive.

'Is Mummy going to die, Aunt Jess?'

Jessica hugged him reassuringly. 'Of course not,' she told him stoutly, 'she just needs to rest. It's hard work looking after Daddy and you. Come on, let's go inside and have some lunch, shall we?'

She suspected that William felt as little like eating as she did herself, but to give way to her own fears in front of her small nephew would not do either of them any good. She longed for Lyle's calming presence at her side, and not just because he was a doctor.

David arrived just as they were finishing lunch, and watching him frown and push William away as he ran to him Jessica could not help contrasting her brother-in-law's attitude to Lyle's.

'What's going on?' he demanded angrily of Jessica. 'I've had to come out of a meeting and come home. Where's Andrea?'

'In hospital,' Jessica told him, not even trying to hide her dislike of him. Andrea, his wife, was lying in hospital quite dangerously ill, and all David seemed concerned about was the fact that he had been called out of his meeting.

She heard him swear and said icily, 'No matter how important your meeting was, David, I'm quite sure it can't be more important than Andrea's life.'

He looked more angry than shocked and Jessica heard him mutter bitterly, 'She's the one who wanted this damned baby, not me.'

Jessica was only thankful that she had had the wit to send William upstairs to clean his teeth, and now she rounded on her brother-in-law, telling him exactly what she thought about him.

'You're a fine one to talk,' he sneered at her. 'The cold-hearted bitch, who married purely to check on her research. Does he know about that yet?'

'No, he doesn't.' She was too angry to pretend

any longer and added curtly, 'And besides, you're wrong. I love him.'

She had the satisfaction of seeing David's eyes widen and then narrow. 'Damn you, Jess,' he swore bitterly, 'damn you for telling me that.' He broke off as they heard a car outside. Jessica recognised the engine note of Lyle's estate car, immediately rushing to the door. Before she got there David stopped her, grabbing hold of her and pulling her into his arms, kissing her brutally before she could push him away.

The front door was open and Lyle walked in just in time to see David releasing her.

Jessica knew quite well how damning the circumstances looked, but she was far too wrought up and angry for excuses and explanations, instead rushing upstairs on the pretext of wanting to check on William.

Instead she went into the spare bedroom, and sat down on the bed taking deep breaths until she was sure she was in control of herself. How could David have kissed her like that when his wife, her sister...? But then she had always suspected that at heart David resented and disliked her, and he had kissed her because he knew how Lyle would interpret their embrace and for no other reason.

More drained than she could ever remember being in her life, Jessica went and found William, taking him downstairs with her.

Lyle was standing in the hall and there was no sign of David. 'We're leaving,' he told Jessica curtly.

She glanced from his set face to William's nervous one, and correctly interpreting her thoughts, Lyle told her icily, 'Chalmers is staying here to look after his son. I've rung the hospital and checked on Andrea. She should be home in a couple of days.'

He waited until they were outside before saying anything more to her, his face a bitter mask of disgust as he ground out, 'My God, the pair of you are despicable. You...'

His contempt Jessica could understand, but his anger frightened her. She could not really see any reason for it, but she was glad that she would not be forced to travel back with him nonetheless.

It was on the journey back that Jessica came to a momentous decision. It was pointless pretending any longer. She was going to have to tell Lyle how she felt and let him make what decision he wished on the continuance or otherwise of their marriage from there. It was simply too much of a strain to continue as they were, and at least he would know then that she had not been using him as a substitute for David as he had once accused her of doing; and that indeed the only feeling she had for her brother-in-law was one of dislike.

She would much rather that Lyle despised her for being stupid enough to fall in love with him than for attempting to break up her sister's marriage, and besides, she was weary of all the pretence, of the growing effort it took to force herself to appear indifferent to him.

He reached the house before her, leaving his car parked untidily across the drive. He got out and strode into the house without waiting for her, and slowly Jessica followed him inside.

He had gone into his office and she followed him there, willing him to look at her.

He did so, his eyes cold with dislike, his forehead pleated in a frown.

'Lyle, I must talk to you.'

'Not now Jessica,' he told her harshly. 'I've got to go out, for which you ought to be thankful. If I had to speak to you now, God knows I don't believe I would be able to control myself. To walk into that house and find you in his arms, your own sister's husband.' His mouth tightened in disgust and a dark rage that totally unnerved her.

'When will you be back?'

'I don't know.' His eyes grew even harder. 'Why do you want to know? Thinking of entertaining your lover here in my absence, are you?'

Now was obviously not the time to tell him the truth. Jessica went upstairs to her own room and stayed there until she heard him drive away, and then she rang Justine to tell her that she was on her way to pick up the boys.

Justine coaxed them into staying on and having tea with her, and it was gone seven o'clock when they eventually arrived back. There was no sign of Lyle, and the strain of waiting for him to come back so that she could talk to him stretched Jessica's already overwound nerves almost to breaking point.

At nine o'clock she rang the hospital and was told that Andrea was improving. At ten-thirty when Lyle had still not come home she went upstairs and ran a bath hoping that it might relax her.

At midnight she was lying in bed, still wide awake, her body waiting tensely for the first sound of his car. It seemed a lifetime before the wide arc of its headlight illuminated her bedroom. Jessica heard him come in and go into the kitchen and then only minutes later she heard him come upstairs and go into his own room.

She had to speak to him tonight. If she didn't she would never sleep. Slipping on her robe she padded across the landing and knocked briefly on his door before going in.

He was lying fully dressed on his bed, thoughtfully contemplating what looked like a full glass of whisky.

'Why so shocked?' he mocked when he saw her expression. 'I'm simply taking a leaf out of your book, although I doubt that I'll be so easily able to forget the events of today.'

'Lyle, please, it wasn't like it seemed.' Jessica

knew she was making a clumsy start, but somehow the sight of Lyle drinking had shocked all her carefully prepared explanations right out of her mind.

Without thinking she went up to him, reaching out pleadingly, but to her anguish he pushed her away, so roughly that she almost fell.

'Don't bother lying to me, Jessica,' he told her harshly. 'I know exactly what it was like. You married me not because of your sister as you told me, but as part of some damned experiment. Your lover told me that much today.'

His words were like a blow to the chest, making her faint with shock and fear.

'David is not my lover,' she said huskily. 'He *never* has been, and he never will be.'

'So you say, but you don't deny what he told me, do you, Jessica. Because you can't.'

How on earth could she explain to Lyle, in his present mood, just why she had told David that? The whole issue was so complex and involved, her own nerves stretched so tensely that she could not trust herself to make him understand.

'Lyle, please.'

'Please what?' he demanded roughly. 'Please make love to you as a substitute for Chalmers?' He laughed harshly. 'My God, you really took me for a fool, didn't you? Well, it's over now, Jessica,' he told her bitterly. 'You can leave this house just as soon as you like.'

Even though she had been expecting them, his words still took her by surprise, shocking her into a paralysis of despair from which she emerged only enough to murmur brokenly, 'But Stuart and James?'

'Oh, yes, you've done your work well on those two, too well. I can't take the risk of what it might do to them if they never see you again, but neither can I endure having you in this house any longer. They're old enough to understand that marriages don't always work out, after all this isn't the first time they've experienced divorce. I won't stop them from seeing you if that's what they want, but I won't have you under my roof any longer, Jessica. By this time tomorrow I want you out, do you understand?' He looked more angry than she had ever seen him before.

Somehow she managed to stagger back to her own room, her life in ruins. He had not even given her an opportunity to defend herself, to explain.

SHE DIDN'T SLEEP. How could she? Her mind went over and over that dreadful scene with Lyle, desperately wishing she had been allowed to explain things, and yet her heart knowing that Lyle had not wanted to hear any explanations. He had wanted to get rid of her.

After breakfast he took her on one side and reiterated, 'I want you out of here just as quickly as possible, please. I'll tell the boys, and I'll be in touch with you to make arrangements for the divorce, and for you to see Stuart and James, if that's what you wish. Please don't say anything to them, I prefer to explain the situation to them myself.'

'So that you can blame me, I suppose,' Jessica flung at him bitterly. 'If only you'd listened, I...'

'You would what? Have told me that your brother-in-law lied when he said you were using our marriage to test out your pet theories? Well?'

How could she explain to him in this mood why she had said that to David? And how odd that he seemed more angry about what was surely only a minor issue than others which to her were far more important.

'Was that why you made love with me?' he demanded harshly. 'As part of an experiment? You'll have to let me know how I rated or will I be able to read about it for myself?'

He came towards her, so angry that for a moment Jessica thought he was going to hit her, and she fell back automatically, watching the rage die from his face, and contempt take its place.

'Oh, for God's sake, I'm not going to touch you,' he told her bitterly. 'I doubt that I could now, even if I wanted to. Why, *why* did you do it?' he demanded thickly. 'Was it because I told you I no longer wanted to make love? Did you find that a challenge you couldn't resist? Was...' He broke off, his mouth snapping shut, and Jessica realised sickly that he was so angry because she had hurt his pride, because he thought she had used him callously and cold-bloodedly. But it was too late to tell him the truth now, too late and of too little importance. He didn't want her in his life any more, in any capacity—he had made that more than clear.

Her flat was let on a monthly tenancy, and for the first week of their separation she lived in a small hotel while waiting for her tenants to quit. Divorce was out of the question in view of the short life of their marriage, but she had received a very curt letter from Lyle telling her that although *he* no longer wished to see her, both boys did and that with her agreement it could be arranged that they would spend their weekends with her.

Jessica was not under any delusion that he did this for her sake—it was only for the sake of the boys themselves that he was allowing her to see them. She swallowed hard. She missed them badly already, and wondered how they had taken her absence. Did they think that she, like their mother, had rejected them?

She longed to ring and speak to them, but pride would not let her. She would not allow Lyle to accuse her of trying to influence the boys behind his back. She had even refused to speak to Justine on the phone, not wanting to make any explanations or

excuses to his sister that might conflict with anything Lyle himself might have to say.

The only good thing that had happened was that
Andrea was now out of hospital. Jessica had kept
from her the news of their separation, not wanting
to cause her sister further anxiety, and had given as
an excuse for asking her not to ring her the fib that
the phone was out of order. Fortunately Andrea was
too caught up in her own affairs to query the danger
of a doctor's phone being in this state.

The first weekend she was alone she spent moving back into her flat which she had let furnished.
That night, for the first time since Lyle had told her
to leave, she slept for two whole hours at a stretch
without waking up.

On Sunday morning when the phone rang, she sat
staring at the receiver for several seconds before
picking it up. Somehow she had known it would be
Lyle, and when he asked if the boys could spend
the day with her she agreed abruptly.

'I'll bring them round at eleven and collect them
again at six.' His voice was so cold that any
thoughts she might have had about trying to explain
to him died at birth.

She saw his car arrive from her sitting-room window, but didn't go down, simply watching as he
directed the boys into the hall and waited as they
pressed her intercom bell.

As she activated the internal locking system to let
them in Jessica saw him drive away. The dull ache

her misery had become over the last few days sharpened acutely, reminding her of all she had lost.

Both boys looked subdued. Her flat was too small for them really, and although it was pleasant enough to go outside, the neatly manicured lawns surrounding the apartments did not tempt one to run about and play on them.

All afternoon Jessica avoided any topic of conversation which might lead to Lyle and the reasons behind the breakdown of their marriage, but half an hour before their father was due to pick them up, Stuart, who had been withdrawn and quiet, flung himself into her arms crying bitterly.

'Why can't you come back with us?' he demanded miserably. 'We miss you. It's horrid at home without you. Why did you leave us, Jessica?'

How on earth could she explain to them without involving their father?

In the end all she could do was hug Stuart tightly, her own tears damping his dark hair as she tried to find a way to explain the impossible.

'Is it because you don't love us any more?' he demanded fiercely at last, pulling away from her and dashing a grubby fist against his eyes.

'No, of course not. I still love you both very, very much,' Jessica reassured him.

'Is it because you don't love Dad, then?'

She had left the window open because of the heat, and Jessica was never more glad to hear the familiar sound of Lyle's car. It hurt dreadfully to send them down to their father, and ignore their pleas to go home with them, but what else could she do? And yet she couldn't find it in her heart to blame Lyle. It would be as difficult for him to explain the situation to them as it was for her.

THE SECOND WEEK of their separation dragged past as painfully as the first. Sleeping and eating were both impossible in her keyed-up state and she knew she was losing weight. Both her skin and hair seemed to have lost their healthy lustre, and the only good thing that had come out of the whole thing was that she had managed to do some work on her book. It was only when she was working that she was able to stop thinking about Lyle—sometimes for almost half an hour at a time, but like all pain killers, work was only effective for so long.

On the Friday she forced herself to go out shopping to buy some food for the weekend, in anticipation of the boys' visit. The phone was ringing as she walked into her flat and she dropped her shopping racing across to pick up the receiver.

'Jessica?'

Even the sound of Lyle's voice was enough to start her heart pounding crazily.

'Yes?'

'I'd like to come round and see you, tonight if possible. We have things to discuss.'

'Yes.'

'I'll be round about seven, then. Susan is going to look after the boys.'

No mention of bringing them round to see her over the weekend, Jessica noted, her whole body gripped by pain as she acknowledged to herself that he might be coming round to tell her that he no longer wanted them to see her. Stuart had been badly upset the previous weekend, and in all fairness they *were* his children and not hers.

Lyle arrived shortly before seven and although she had been waiting for this moment all day, now that he was here Jessica felt unable to cope with seeing him.

Even so she let him in, standing back so that he could precede her into the small sitting-room.

She offered him a drink and watched him shake his head, his mouth compressing, his voice harsh as he said, 'No, thanks.'

He wouldn't sit down, going instead to stand in front of the window, with his back to her, his hands jammed into the pockets of his jeans. His whole body betrayed his tension, and Jessica could easily imagine how difficult it was for him to see her when he despised her so much.

'Why have you come to see me, Lyle?' she asked him unevenly when several seconds had gone by without his saying a word. 'Is it about the boys? Stuart was dreadfully upset last weekend.' Her voice expressed her own pain, and he swung round, look-ing at her with hard eyes, his voice grim, as he said curtly, 'I've decided to send them to boarding-school once the holidays are over. It seems the best solution all round.' He saw her anguished expression and smiled mirthlessly. 'You should have thought about that before, Jessica.'

His bitterness stung, making her want to lash out and hurt him as he had hurt her.

'Just as you should have thought about them instead of giving all your love to Heather,' she retaliated bitterly.

'All my love?' He laughed harshly. 'My God, where did you get that idea? I stopped loving Heather, if I ever did, when I realised how different she was from my foolish adolescent image of her. And besides, you're a fine one to talk. What about Chalmers?'

Driven to the point of explosion Jessica told him fiercely, 'For the last time, David means *nothing* to me and *never* has done. I *loathe* him and always have done. That's why I told him I was marrying you as an experiment. I wanted to get it through that impenetrable ego of his just how little he meant to me.'

'Then you didn't marry me simply to use our relationship as the basis for an experiment?'

'No, of course not. I *am* human, you know, Lyle,' she cried out, painfully tormented by his cross-questioning and not able to see what benefit it could be to either of them now. 'I married you for the reason I gave you at the time. It did briefly cross

my mind that in entering into such a marriage I
would be in an ideal position to see how justified I
was in claiming that a marriage could be successful
and long-standing without being based on romantic
love, but that wasn't the reason I married you.

'Why have you come to see me?' she demanded
wearily. 'I really am very tired, and so far you
haven't said anything that you couldn't have said
over the telephone. I do wish, though, that you
wouldn't send the boys to boarding-school.'

'There's only one way I can avoid doing that.'

He had his back to her again, but his face was
visible to her in profile and she watched in bemused
misery as a tiny muscle flickered betrayingly against
his jaw.

'How?'

'If you agree to come back.'

It was the very last thing she had expected to hear;
and she could hardly take in the fact that after the
way he had demanded that she leave, Lyle was now
asking her to come back.

She had always known that he loved the boys, of
course, but she had not realised to what extent, and
she felt both pain and compassion for him as she
stared at his rigid back.

'Well, Jessica, what is it to be? Will you come
back? If you do I'm prepared to overlook everything
that's happened, the fact that I discovered you in
Chalmers' arms…and you were, despite what you
say about your feelings towards him.'

Suddenly something inside her snapped, releasing a flood of bitter emotion.

'Oh, that's *very* generous of you,' she told him in a strained high voice, 'but tell me this, Lyle, are you also able to overlook the fact that I've fallen in love with you? Because I'm afraid that I have, and if you can't...'

She turned her back on him, knowing that he must leave now, that he would not want her back, living under the same roof with him now that she had told him the truth.

The shock of having his hands descend on her shoulders and turn her very ungently to face him, gripping her arms tightly as he looked down into her eyes, made the room swing dizzily around her.

Colour burned under his skin, his eyes so dark that they looked more black than blue. He was sweating slightly, his voice a hoarse cry of disbelief as he demanded rawly, 'What are you saying, Jessica?'

She wasn't going to back down now. Stubbornly refusing to give in to her own anguish, she said huskily, 'I'm saying that if I come back to live with you, it must be without any pretence between us, Lyle. I love you. I admit love is an emotion I never expected to feel, hardly believed actually existed between adults. I'd convinced myself during my research and from my own observation of life that what we call love is more often merely physical lust, and as such doesn't stand up to the test of time, but now I know I was wrong. I'm not asking you to love me in return—I know that's impossible. But if I come back it must be in the knowledge that you are aware of my feelings. I can't live a lie any longer.'

'Neither can I.' The harshness had gone from his voice, leaving it faintly raw as though he had scraped his throat. 'I didn't come here to ask you to come back because of the boys at all,' he told her huskily. 'I came because *I* couldn't endure another day without you. You'll never know how bitterly I've regretted giving in to my jealousy of Chalmers. I wanted you to *deny* that he meant anything to you, and I have done ever since that night we first made love. I knew then how important you were to me, but I tried to resist it. I told myself it was him you wanted not me, that you were just using me as a substitute.'

'I can't believe this,' Jessica whispered, staring at him. 'I can't believe you love me.'

'Can't you?' He made a thick, impassioned sound of anguish in his throat and then said, 'Then what the hell am I supposed to call this?' With such suppressed violence that Jessica actually shivered in response to it, he almost jerked off her feet as he took her in his arms.

She could feel him trembling, feel the emotion building up inside him, as he kissed her with a starving passion.

It could have been seconds or hours before he

released her, her body so light and empty that she almost fell.

'And if you dare to call that lust, or anger, I think I shall probably kill you,' Lyle told her softly. 'Jessica, Jessica...' He took her back in his arms, kissing her eyelids, probing the trembling outline of her mouth with his thumb until she gasped and shivered with desire, turning her face up to his and abandoning herself to the heat of his mouth.

This time he released her slowly, savouring the sweetness of her mouth as he did so.

'You'll never know what it's cost me in sleepless nights to come here today,' he told her softly. 'I've been rejected once by a woman I thought I loved, and I still bear the scars, but I knew today that life without you was so meaningless, that whatever pain I risked was nothing compared with the misery my life would be without you in it.'

As she listened to him Jessica realised what an effort it had been for him it to come to her, having endured, as he had just said, one traumatic rejection from Heather.

If she had needed confirmation that he genuinely loved her she had just received it. To get her back he had been prepared to humble himself completely, to take her back on any terms, just as she would have gone back.

'We've been very lucky, you and I,' he murmured into her hair. 'To have been given this chance to love one another, especially in view of the inauspicious way in which we met.'

'Mmm, it does pose a problem, though,' Jessica mused, closing her eyes and moving closer to the hard outline of his body, 'at least as far as my book's concerned. Was love the cause of our marriage or the result of it? Were we attracted to one another when we first met to such an extent that we both found excuses to go through with the marriage, or did it grow after we were married?'

His mouth silenced her, taking hers in a sensually demanding kiss. When he eventually raised his head to smile down into her flushed face he asked softly, 'Does it really matter?'

Jessica shook her head. 'Not in the least. What does matter is that there is love.'

'Is now and always will be,' Lyle affirmed, adding as his lips caressed her skin, 'you do realise that Justine is really going to be full of herself now, don't you?'

But it seemed he wasn't expecting an answer, because his mouth was already taking the breath from her own, telling her in a way more satisfactory than any words the truth of what he had already said: that there was love and always would be.

Harlequin Romance®

Delightful

Affectionate

Romantic

Emotional

Tender

Original

Daring

Riveting

Enchanting

Adventurous

Moving

**Harlequin Romance—the
series that has it all!**

HROM-G